進階英文 上

鄧慧君 編著

三民書局

網際網路位址　http : // www. sanmin. com. tw

ⓒ　進階英文（上）

編著者　鄧慧君
發行人　劉振強
著作財　三民書局股份有限公司
產權人　臺北市復興北路三八六號
發行所　三民書局股份有限公司
　　　　地址／臺北市復興北路三八六號
　　　　電話／二五〇〇六六〇〇
　　　　郵撥／〇〇〇九九九八──五號
印刷所　三民書局股份有限公司
門市部　復北店／臺北市復興北路三八六號
　　　　重南店／臺北市重慶南路一段六十一號
初　版　中華民國八十九年八月
編　號　S 80358

行政院新聞局登記證局版臺業字第〇二〇〇號

ISBN　957-14-3239-3　（平裝）

前　言

　　本書係針對具有基礎英文能力之學生所設計的教材,目標在提供進階英文能力之訓練,及科技人文相關內容知識之吸取。

　　選文方面以「生活化、趣味化、多元化」為原則,配合每課之主題,均有一篇課文及一篇課外閱讀。每課包含詞類變化 (Word Forms) 及句型練習 (Sentence Patterns) 兩部份,配合課文中出現的例字、例句,讓學生從語境中作即時的練習,以增強學習效果。其次,習題 (Exercise) 中的 Discussion Topics 部份,提供教師與課文內容相關的一些課題,使學生能將本身的經驗與課文連接在一起,作為課堂討論或寫作練習之參考。此外,每課的課外閱讀 (Outside Reading) 部份,由教師依上課時間之多寡,可於課堂中講授,或指定學生自行研讀,並可藉由 Reading Comprehension,檢視學生理解的程度。最後,每課後面附有英語學習策略 (English Learning Strategy),透過淺顯易懂的圖文介紹,使學生的英文學習達到「事半功倍」的最佳效果。

　　本書雖精心編纂,但仍難免有疏漏之處,尚請方家讀者,不吝指正。

鄧慧君　謹誌

2000 年 5 月

略語表

Adj.	形容詞
Adv.	副詞
Aux.	助動詞
[C]	可數
Conj.	連接詞
Int.	感嘆詞
N.	名詞
N.P.	名詞片語
O.	受詞
O.C.	受詞補語
P.P.	過去分詞
Prep.	介系詞
Pron.	代名詞
S.	主詞
S.C.	主詞補語
[U]	不可數
V.	（原形）動詞
Vi.	不及物動詞
V-ing	現在分詞、動名詞
V.P.	動詞片語
Vt.	及物動詞

Contents

Acknowledgements

Texts

◎Home Shopping TV Networks: The Wave of the Future?

From SPECTRUM 4 by Diane Warshawsky, Donald R. H. Byrd, David Rein and Nancy Frankfort, published by Prentice-Hall, Inc. Copyright © 1994. Reprinted by permission of the publisher.

◎Shopping for Bargains

From PROJECT ACHIEVEMENT: READING D by George D. Spache and Evelyn B. Spache, published by Scholastic Inc. Copyright © 1984. Reprinted by permission of the publisher.

◎Traveling by Computer

From KALEIDOSCOPE 1 by Sokmen, Anita and Daphne Mackey, published by Houghton Mifflin Company. Copyright © 1998. Reprinted by permission of the publisher.

◎Welcome to the Web

From THE WORLD WIDE WEB by Christopher Lampton, published by Franklin Watts, a division of Grolier Publishing. Copyright © 1997. Reprinted by permission of the publisher.

◎Earthquake in L.A.

Written by Rick Gore, published in the April 1995 issue of NATIONAL GEOGRAPHIC MAGAZINE. Reprinted by permission of National Geographic Magazine.

◎Tornadoes

From ALL ABOUT THE USA, A CULTURAL READER by Milada Broukal and Peter Murphy, published by Addison Wesley Longman. Copyright © 1991.

◎Thanksgiving Days

From AUTUMN FESTIVALS by Mike Rosen, published by Wayland (Publishers) Limited. Copyright © 1990. Reprinted by permission of the publisher.

◎Who Really Discovered America?

From PROJECT ACHIEVEMENT: READING A by George D. Spache and Evelyn B. Spache, published by Scholastic Inc. Copyright © 1982. Reprinted by permission of the publisher.

◎Fictional Heroes Never Die

From MOVE UP by Simon Greenall, published by Heinemann Publishers (Oxford) Ltd. Copyright © 1995. Reprinted by permission of Heinemann Educational Publishers, a division of Reed Educational & Professional Publishing Ltd.

◎The Beatles

From THINKING ENGLISH by Michael Thorn, published by Cassell Ltd, Wellington House, 125 Strand, London, England. Copyright © 1982. Reprinted by permission of the publisher.

◎Christmas Traditions

From WINTER FESTIVALS by Mike Rosen, published by Wayland (Publishers) Limited. Copyright © 1990. Reprinted by permission of the publisher.

◎Valentine's Day

Rewritten by Michael Jeaques.

◎Time Difference

From SEEING MORE OF THE WORLD by Alan Turney and Yasuo Kawabe, published by Seibido Publishing Co., Ltd. Copyright © 1990. Reprinted by permission of the publisher.

◎Procrastination

From LADO ENGLISH SERIES 5 by Robert Lado, published by Prentice-Hall, Inc., Upper Saddle River, NJ. Copyright © 1990. Reprinted by permission of the publisher.

◎Answering Machines

From COMMUNICATOR II by Steven J. Molinsky and Bill Bliss, published by Prentice-Hall, Inc., Upper Saddle River, NJ. Copyright ©1995. Reprinted by permission of the publisher.

◎Always Return Your Phone Calls

From CHICKEN SOUP FOR THE TEENAGE SOUL by Jack Canfield, Mark Victor Hansen and Kimberly Kirberger, published by Health Communications, Inc. Copyright © 1997.

Photographs

pp.1, 3, 12, 77　李憲章

pp.30, 31, 43, 49　美聯社

p.61 James Bond, Batman, Bugs Bunny, Kermit　Aquarius Picture Library
　　　Charlie Brown　PEANUTS © United Feature Syndicate, Inc.

p.73　Aquarius Picture Library

pp.78, 80　薛聰賢

p.79　天主教聖家堂

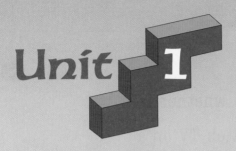

Unit 1

Home Shopping TV Networks:
The Wave of the Future?

Have you ever watched a home shopping program on TV? Can you describe what it's like to shop at home by television?

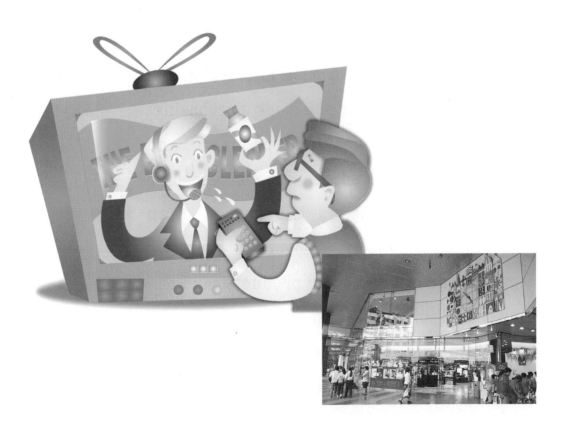

Have you ever had to decide whether to go shopping or stay home and watch TV on a weekend? Now you can do both *at the same time*. Home shopping television **networks**[1] have become a way for many people to shop without ever *having to* leave their homes.

Some shoppers *are tired of* department stores and shopping **malls**[2]—fighting the **crowds**,[3] waiting in long lines, and sometimes not even finding anything they want to buy. They'd rather sit quietly at home *in front of* the TV set and watch a friendly **announcer**[4] describe an item while a model **displays**[5] it. And they can shop *around the clock*, **purchasing**[6] an item simply by making a phone call and **charging**[7] it to a credit card. Home shopping networks understand the power of an **enthusiastic**[8] host, the **glamour**[9] of **celebrity**[10] guests **endorsing**[11] their products, and the emotional pull of a **bargain**.[12]

Major fashion designers, department stores, and even **mail-order**[13] **catalogue**[14]

network [ˈnɛt,wɝk]

mall [mɔl]

crowd [kraʊd]

announcer [əˈnaʊnsɚ]

display [dɪˈsple]

purchase [ˈpɝtʃəs]

charge [tʃɑrdʒ]

enthusiastic

  [ɪn,θjuzɪˈæstɪk]

glamour [ˈɡlæmɚ]

celebrity [səˈlɛbrətɪ]

endorse [ɪnˈdɔrs]

bargain [ˈbɑrɡɪn]

mail-order [ˈmel,ɔrdɚ]

catalogue [ˈkætl,ɔɡ]

companies are eager to *join in* the success of home shopping. Large department stores are experimenting with their own TV channels, and some retailers are planning to introduce **interactive**[15] TV shopping in the future. Then, viewers will be able to communicate with their own personal shoppers, asking questions about products and placing orders, all through their TV sets.

Will shopping by television **replace**[16] shopping in stores? Some industry **executives**[17] claim that home shopping networks represent the "electronic shopping mall of the future." Yet for many people, going out and shopping at a real store is a way to relax and even be entertained. And for many shoppers, it is still important to touch or *try on* items they want to buy. That's why experts say that *in the future*, home shopping will exist **alongside**[18] store shopping but will never **entirely**[19] replace it.

25

30

35

40

interactive

[ˌɪntɚˈæktɪv]

replace [rɪˈples]

executive [ɪgˈzɛkjutɪv]

alongside [əˈlɔŋˈsaɪd]

entirely [ɪnˈtaɪrlɪ]

A. Vocabulary

1. **network** [ˈnɛt,wɝk] *n.* [C] a group of broadcasting stations connected for the simultaneous broadcast of a program 廣播網

   The beauty contest was broadcast on a TV *network*.

2. **mall** [mɔl] *n.* [C] a shopping center 購物中心

   I met Judy and her boyfriend at the *mall* yesterday.

3. **crowd** [kraʊd] *n.* [C] a large gathering of people 人群

   There was a large *crowd* of people in the airport.

4. **announcer** [əˈnaʊnsɚ] *n.* [C] a person who announces in broadcasting 播音員

   "That's the end of broadcasting for today," the *announcer* said. "So good night, my dear audience."

5. **display** [dɪˈsple] *vt.* to exhibit; show 展示；陳列

   Various styles of shoes are *displayed* in the shopwindows.

6. **purchase** [ˈpɝtʃəs] *vt.* to buy 購買

   Ms. Lin usually *purchases* food in the supermarket near her house.

7. **charge** [tʃardʒ] *vt.* to debit the cost to an account 賒購；記帳

   Please *charge* the cost to my account.

8. **enthusiastic** [ɪn,θjuzɪˈæstɪk] *adj.* having great eagerness 狂熱的

   Jeff is *enthusiastic* about professional basketball.

9. **glamour** [ˈglæmɚ] *n.* [U] exciting charm; physical attractiveness 魅力

   Elvis is an actor of great *glamour*.

10. **celebrity** [sə'lɛbrətɪ] *n.* [C] a famous person 名人

    A lot of *celebrities* have eaten in the restaurant.

11. **endorse** [ɪn'dɔrs] *vt.* to recommend 推薦

    This product has been *endorsed* by many housewives.

12. **bargain** ['bɑrgɪn] *n.* [C] a cheap price 廉價

    Jane bought the coat at a *bargain*.

13. **mail-order** ['mel,ɔrdɚ] *adj.* purchasing goods by post 郵購的

    There are more *mail-order* firms in Taiwan than ever before.

14. **catalogue** ['kætl̩,ɔg] *n.* [C] a list 目錄

    This article is put in a *catalogue*.

15. **interactive** [,ɪntɚ'æktɪv] *adj.* allowing a two-way flow of
    information between a device and its user 交互作用的

    It is crucial for computer software to have an *interactive* function.

16. **replace** [rɪ'ples] *vt.* to take the place of 取代

    Radios have been *replaced* by televisions.

17. **executive** [ɪg'zɛkjutɪv] *n.* [C] a person with managerial or administrative
    responsibility 經營者；管理者

    Thomas became the *executive* of this company as a result of his hard working.

18. **alongside** [ə'lɔŋ'saɪd] *prep.* close to the side of 靠著…旁邊

    You can park your car *alongside* mine.

19. **entirely** [ɪn'taɪrlɪ] *adv.* completely 完全地

    She is *entirely* devoted to folk dancing.

B. Idioms & Phrases

1. **at the same time** simultaneously 同時

   John usually watches television and eats his dinner *at the same time*.

2. **have to** must 必須

   We *have to* get up early to catch the train.

3. **be tired of** to be bored with something 厭倦

   The Smith family *were tired of* the big city and moved into a small town.

4. **in front of** before 在⋯之前

   There used to be a tree *in front of* the house.

5. **around the clock** for twenty-four hours without stopping 不眠不休地

   The police watched the house *around the clock* but no one showed up.

6. **join in** to participate in 加入

   You can *join in* our baseball team if you have time.

7. **try on** to put on (clothes etc.) to see if they fit 試穿（戴）

   You can *try on* the jeans in the dressing room.

8. **in the future** in time to come 在將來

   Helen's parents want her to study abroad *in the future*.

C. Word Forms

1. | v. + -er → n. |

shop（購物）	→	shopper（購物者）
announce（播報）	→	announcer（播音員）
design（設計）	→	designer（設計師）
retail（零售）	→	retailer（零售商）
view（觀看）	→	viewer（觀眾）

 Enthusiastic **consumers** of fruit are very demanding. They want only the freshest fruit.

They **consume** tons of fruit every year.

2. **n. + -al → adj.**

emotion（情緒）	→	emotional（情緒的）
person（個人）	→	personal（私人的）

 The design for a car that operates on solar energy is in the **experimental** stage.

Researchers will need to perform dozens of **experiments** to perfect this car.

 牛刀小試

1. Like other _____ (employ), she wanted experienced people who didn't need much training.

2. John is a very dependable _____ (work).

3. Mark does not _____ (grow) flowers in his garden. He only plants vegetables.

D. Sentence Patterns

1. **S. + V.P. + without + V-ing**

 Many people shop **without** ever **having** to leave their homes.

    (1) She left **without saying** good-bye to me.

    (2) John entered the school **without having** to take an entrance exam.

    (3) He committed a crime **without being** caught.

2. **S. + would rather + 原形 V.（寧願）**

 They **'d rather sit** quietly at home in front of the TV set.

（註：口語常用 'd rather）

    (1) I **would rather stay** at home.

    (2) I **would rather** not **go** out.

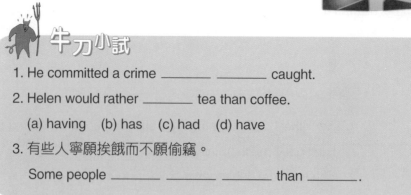

牛刀小試

  1. He committed a crime _____ _____ caught.

  2. Helen would rather _____ tea than coffee.

    (a) having   (b) has   (c) had   (d) have

  3. 有些人寧願挨餓而不願偷竊。

    Some people _____ _____ _____ than _____.

E. Exercise

I. True/False: *Decide true (T) or false (F) of the following statements based on the text.*

❶ Shoppers often find anything they want to buy in department stores and shopping malls.

❷ People can shop around the clock by home shopping networks.

❸ There will be interactive TV shopping in the future.

❹ A lot of people still enjoy going out and shopping.

❺ Store shopping will be completely replaced by home shopping in the future.

II. Vocabulary Review: *Complete the sentences with the following words of appropriate forms.*

personal	order	replace	describe	experiment
claim	fashion	shopping	introduce	display

❶ Please _____ the circumstances in detail.

❷ Joe _____ that he was innocent.

❸ May I take your _____ , sir?

❹ They are _____ on animals with a new medicine.

❺ Nowadays many students own _____ computers.

❻ The wise do their Christmas _____ in October.

❼ All the old computers have been _____ by new ones.

❽ A great _____ of fireworks took place last evening.

❾ Western culture was _____ into China.

❿ She dresses in the height of the _____ .

III. Multiple Choice: *Choose the most appropriate word based on the meaning of the context.*

❶ I don't know whether he is at home _____ at school.

(a) and   (b) or   (c) but   (d) as

❷ That strange girl left _____ saying good-bye.

(a) for   (b) about   (c) on   (d) without

❸ They have studied _____ the clock to prepare the entrance exam held the next day.

(a) around   (b) like   (c) against   (d) by

❹ Scientists are experimenting _____ new medicine for the treatment of AIDS.

(a) with   (b) on   (c) in   (d) about

❺ Some stores do not allow customers to _____ on clothes on sale.

(a) get   (b) take   (c) try   (d) turn

IV. Cloze Test: *Fill in the blanks with the most appropriate words based on the meaning of the context.*

Home shopping television networks have become a way for many people to shop ^{1}_____ ever having to leave their homes. Some shoppers are ^{2}_____ of department stores and shopping malls. They'd ^{3}_____ sit quietly at home in front of the TV set and watch a friendly announcer describe an item while a model ^{4}_____ it. And they can purchase an item simply by ^{5}_____ a phone call and charging it to a ^{6}_____ card. Home shopping networks understand the power of an enthusiastic ^{7}_____ , and the glamour of celebrity guests endorsing their products.

V. Translation: *Translate the following Chinese sentences into English.*

❶ 你是否曾在週末猶豫究竟該出門採購亦或待在家裡看電視呢？

_____

❷ 電視購物將會取代商店購物嗎？

_____

❸ 有些購物者厭倦百貨公司及購物中心。

_____

❹ 購物者只要打電話便能購買物品。

_____

❺ 甚至郵購公司渴望加入家庭購物的成功。

_____

VI. Discussion Topics: *Discuss the following topics on "shopping" in oral or written reports.*

❶ Have you ever watched a home shopping program on TV? Do you think it's a good way to shop? Why or why not?

❷ Do you prefer home shopping or store shopping? Explain your answer.

❸ Please describe the most unforgettable shopping experience of yours.

Outside Reading

Shopping for Bargains

Few people can resist a bargain. But bargains are not always what they seem. Some sales and bargains are good deals, but not all are. Here are some pointers to help you tell the difference between real bargains and bad deals.

Sometimes a product is on sale for "below manufacturer's cost." Watch out for this kind of "bargain." Why would anyone want to sell a product for less than it cost to make it? Before buying, you should find out why it is being sold at a loss to the manufacturer. Is it damaged? Is it out of style? Does it come with any guarantee?

Another pointer is to read price tags on sale items carefully. For example, a price tag in a store may say "regular price $16." The regular price is the price of the item before the sale started and after the sale ends. The regular price is only for that store, however. In another store, the price could be lower.

A price tag may also say "original price $16." That means at one time the item sold for $16—even as much as five years earlier! For example, the original price of pocket calculators was high when they were introduced. Now the price is much lower. Showing the original price would be misleading.

Finally, be careful how you use cents-off coupons. A coupon can save you money only if you intend to use the item. The price of an item may vary at different stores, so use the coupon at the store with the lowest price. Don't forget to add any sales tax to the item before you figure out the "cents-off" price.

Reading Comprehension

1. According to the author, _____ are good deals.

   (a) all sales   (b) some bargains   (c) no bargains

2. Customers should watch out for the bargain when a product is on sale for below _____ .

   (a) regular price   (b) manufacturer's cost (c) original price

3. One pointer to help customers tell the difference between real bargains and bad deals is to read _____ on sale items carefully.

   (a) price tags   (b) cents-off coupons   (c) product descriptions

4. To save money, the author suggests that customers use the coupon at the store _____ .

   (a) near their home   (b) with the lowest price   (c) with the best service

5. Which is NOT included in the possible reasons for a product sold less than it cost to make it?

   (a) It is out of style.   (b) It is damaged.   (c) It is popular.

English Learning Strategy

Use new English words in a sentence in order to remember them. (將英文生字放進句子中使用,以便記住生字。)

Unit  2

Traveling by Computer

*Computers are rapidly changing our lives and opening doors to the rest of the world. This reading describes the revolutionary changes created by **electronic**[1] mail.*

    Electronic mail, or "e-mail," is causing a **revolution**² in our lives just as the telephone did. It is changing the way we **communicate**³ with *one another*. This speedy, **informal**⁴
5   means of communication is becoming more and more popular among all age groups around the world. To use it, all you need is a computer, communications software, a **modem**,⁵ and a phone line. Once you have an e-mail **address**,⁶
10 you can "talk" to people *all over* the world. Millions of people have e-mail addresses.

    Why is e-mail becoming more popular than **regular**,⁷ or "*snail*," *mail*? First of all, it's fast. You can send your **message**⁸ in seconds
15 *instead of* days. In addition, e-mail is cheaper than regular mail. You are using your telephone line, but the cost is much lower than the cost of regular calls on your telephone bill. E-mail is also very convenient.
20 It is easy to use because you and the other person don't have to be on the line at the same time. You can write your message

electronic [ɪˌlɛk'tranɪk]

revolution [ˌrɛvə'luʃən]

communicate
  [kə'mjunəˌket]

informal [ɪn'fɔrml]

modem ['modɛm]

address [ə'drɛs, 'ædrɛs]

regular ['rɛgjələ˞]

message ['mɛsɪdʒ]

save [sev]

account [əˈkaʊnt]

doorway [ˈdorˌwe]

current [ˈkɝənt]

zone [zon]

border [ˈbɔrdɚ]

when you have time. The other person can read it when he or she has time. You can start to write a message, **save**[9] it, and continue it later. You can print messages and save them. E-mail is also good for the environment: It uses no trees, no paper, and no gasoline!

Finally, your e-mail **account**[10] is your **doorway**[11] to the Internet, a "superhighway" of millions of interconnected computers. You can find books, journals, information, computer software, and even whole libraries from around the world there. You can get the **current**[12] news, sports results, and weather information. You can also "meet" people and discuss topics you*'re interested in.* Another attraction is that everyone is equal on e-mail. You can't see how people look or how much money they have. The written word is popular again. Your own words and ideas are important. With your e-mail account, you will become a traveler in a world without time **zones**[13] or **borders**.[14]

25

30

35

40

A . Vocabulary

1. **electronic** [ɪ,lɛk'trɑnɪk] *adj.* produced by or involving the flow of electrons 電子的

   Nowadays many people prefer sending *electronic* cards rather than traditional cards.

2. **revolution** [,rɛvə'luʃən] *n.* [C] any fundamental change or reversal of conditions 革新

   Computer technology has caused a *revolution* in business practices.

3. **communicate** [kə'mjunə,ket] *vi.* to impart or transmit (news, heat, motion, feelings, disease, ideas, etc.) 溝通

   The clerk learnt how to use sign language to *communicate* with deaf customers.

4. **informal** [ɪn'fɔrml] *adj.* not formal 非正式的

   Most of the time Cathy wears *informal* clothes.

5. **modem** ['modɛm] *n.* [C] a device which uses a telephone line to connect computers or computer system 數據機

   Jack sent an e-mail to his teacher by *modem*.

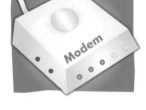

6. **address** [ə'drɛs, 'ædrɛs] *n.* [C] a place where a person lives or an organization is situated 地址

   The *address* on this envelope is not clear.

7. **regular** ['rɛgjələ] *adj.* ordinary, without any special feature or qualities 正規的

   Regular teachers don't have the training to deal with learning-disable students.

8. **message** ['mɛsɪdʒ] *n.* [C] communication sent by one person to another　信息

   I received a *message* from my parents yesterday.

9. **save** [sev] *vt.* to keep for future use　儲存

   You can *save* the message in this disk.

10. **account** [ə'kaʊnt] *n.* [C] an arrangement that you have with a bank to pay in or take out money　帳戶

    Some banks make it difficult to open an *account*.

11. **doorway** ['dor,we] *n.* [C] an opening filled by a door　（通往⋯的）門戶

    I looked up to see David standing in the *doorway*.

12. **current** ['kɝ·ənt] *adj.* belonging to the present; happening now　現時的

    The *current* situation is very different from that in 1980.

13. **zone** [zon] *n.* [C] an area having particular features, properties, purpose, or use　區域

    The north side of this country has virtually become a war *zone*.

14. **border** ['bɔrdɚ] *n.* [C] a line or region separating two countries　國界

    The airplane has flown across the *border*.

B. Idioms & Phrases

1. **one another**　each other or others　互相

   The girls are talking to *one another*.

2. **all over**　in or on all parts of　遍及⋯各地

   The students said they had cleaned up but there was garbage *all over* the place.

3. **snail mail**　letters that are sent by post　平信

Some computer users refer to the postal system as *snail mail*, because it is very slow compared with e-mail system.

4. **instead of** as an alternative 代替…

We learned English *instead of* Japanese.

5. **be interested in** to cause (a person) to take a personal interest 對…感興趣

Victor *is interested in* playing computer games.

C. Word Forms

1. $\text{v.} + \begin{cases} \text{-ion} \\ \text{-ation} \end{cases} \rightarrow \text{n.}$

revolute（革新）	→	revolution（革新）
communicate（溝通）	→	communication（溝通）
inform（通知）	→	information（訊息）
attract（吸引）	→	attraction（吸引力）

 The teacher is ***informing*** us about the TOEFL right now.

This ***information*** will be very helpful to all of us.

2. **n. + -y → adj.**

speed（速度）	→	speedy（快速的）
wind（風）	→	windy（多風的）

It **_rains_** a lot recently.

It is a **_rainy_** day today.

 牛刀小試

1. If there are only a few _____ (correct), the students get good grades.
2. The doctor's _____ (examine) of the sick child will take a long time.
3. What a beautiful _____ (sun) day!

 D. **Sentence Patterns**

1. | S. + V.P. + more + Adj. + than + N.P. (+ V.P.) （比…，較…）

 Why is e-mail becoming **_more_** popular **_than_** regular, or "snail," mail?

(1) Jackson is **_more_** handsome **_than_** Tom.

(2) The cookies made by Mom are **_more_** delicious **_than_** those made by stores.

2. | S. + V.P. + instead of + { N.P. / V-ing （不…而改）

You can send your message in seconds **_instead of_** days.

(1) They had meat **_instead of_** fish for dinner.

(2) He went to the meeting **_instead of_** his wife.

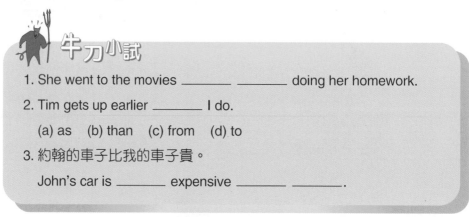

牛刀小試

1. She went to the movies _____ _____ doing her homework.

2. Tim gets up earlier _____ I do.

   (a) as   (b) than   (c) from   (d) to

3. 約翰的車子比我的車子貴。

   John's car is _____ expensive _____ _____.

. **Exercise**

I. True/False: *Decide true (T) or false (F) of the following statements based on the text.*

❶ E-mail is becoming more and more popular only among young people around the world.

❷ E-mail is cheaper than regular mail.

❸ When communicating by e-mail, you and the other person have to be on the line at the same time.

❹ E-mail is good for the environment because it uses no paper.

❺ The written words are no more important with the popularity of e-mail.

II. Vocabulary Review: *Complete the sentences with the following words of appropriate forms.*

telephone	address	send	informal	cost
message	continue	zone	environment	popular

❶ I have _____ letters to all my friends.

❷ Professor Smith is _____ among the students.

❸ May I use your _____ ?

❹ The _____ of the war in lives and property was great.

❺ He _____ reading, ignoring the bell.

❻ Let me know if you change your _____ .

❼ Professors of social problems investigate the home, social, and moral _____ of different classes of people.

❽ There will be an _____ presentation before the due date of this project.

❾ My parents have not had a _____ from my brother for nearly a month.

❿ New Zealand and Taiwan are in different time _____ .

III. Multiple Choice: *Choose the most appropriate word based on the meaning of the context.*

❶ The girls looked all _____ for the key.

    (a) with   (b) of (c) about   (d) over

❷ My sister decided to study in that private university instead _____ the public university near our home.

    (a) of   (b) as (c) for   (d) by

❸ Are you interested _____ reading novels?

    (a) at   (b) on (c) in   (d) of

❹ Do you want to go shopping _____ go swimming?

    (a) and   (b) or (c) but   (d) so

❺ Ken wants to buy the new apartment, _____ his wife does not agree with him.

    (a) but   (b) and   (c) or (d) for

IV. Cloze Test: *Fill in the blanks with the most appropriate words based on the meaning of the context.*

    Why is e-mail becoming more popular than [1]_____ , or "snail," mail? First of all, it's fast. You can [2]_____ your message in seconds instead of days. In

³_____ , e-mail is cheaper than regular mail. You are using your telephone ⁴_____ , but the cost is much lower than the cost of regular calls on your telephone ⁵_____ . E-mail is also very convenient. It is easy to use because you and the other person don't have to be on the line at the same time. You can write your ⁶_____ when you have time. The other person can ⁷_____ it when he or she has time.

V. Translation: *Translate the following Chinese sentences into English.*

❶ 電子郵件正在改變著我們彼此溝通的方式。

_____

❷ 一旦你擁有一個電子郵件地址，你便可以和全世界的人「講話」。

_____

❸ 你的電子郵件帳戶是你通往網際網路的門戶。

_____

❹ 你無法看到人們的長相或是他們擁有多少財富。

_____

❺ 藉由你的電子郵件帳戶，你將不受時差的限制，成為環遊世界的旅行者。

_____

VI. Discussion Topics: *Discuss the following topics on "e-mail" in oral or written reports.*

❶ What are the advantages of e-mail?

❷ Please compare the four different ways of communication, i.e., "face to face," telephone, letter, and e-mail. Which one do you prefer?

❸ Please describe your personal experience on e-mail or BBS.

Outside Reading

Welcome to the Web

Would you like to go to a place where you can see scenes from the latest movies, play games with people from all around the world, and get free versions of brand new computer programs?

If you go to this place, you might meet characters from the latest cartoons, hear samples of songs that haven't even come out yet, or learn the news before it appears on TV. Or, if you prefer, you can browse through museums, admiring beautiful paintings or statues of dinosaurs. You can look out the window of the space shuttle, listen to radio stations on the other side of the country, and even collect photographs of your favorite TV stars.

What is this place? It's called the *World Wide Web*. Like a giant book, the Web is full of pictures and words, but you'll find a lot of things you've never seen in a book before, such as animated cartoons and computer programs. And you get there, believe it or not, through a computer.

The Internet

The World Wide Web is part of the international computer network called the *Internet*. What is the Internet? In a sense, it's just a bunch of wires and cables connecting millions of computers around the world. That may not sound very exciting in itself, but the Internet allows people all over the world to

exchange exciting information quickly and inexpensively. By hooking your own computer to this network of wires through the telephone lines attached to your house, or by using special computers at your school or the local library, you can connect right to the Internet yourself.

And then you can be a part of the World Wide Web!

Computer Files

Once you have a computer that's connected to the Internet, you can use special computer programs to exchange information with other computers connected to the Internet. What kind of information can you send back and forth? Anything that can be stored on a computer—documents, games, sounds, pictures, and programs—can be sent over the Internet.

All the information stored on your computer is arranged in *data files*. Your favorite computer game, the word processing program you use to type your homework, even the homework you create with that word processing program are stored in data files. The data files are recorded on the surface of a disk, which may be a portable diskette or the permanent disk inside your *hard drive*, where they can be retrieved whenever you need them.

The files you find on the Internet are exactly like the files you have on the hard drive of your computer. Like the files on your computer, they can contain many different types of information: computer programs, stories, pictures, even music. But there are more files on the Internet than you could ever fit on your computer. Remember, these files are actually kept on the hard drives of computers all around the world!

Reading Comprehension

1. People can _____ on the web.

   (a) get free versions of brand new computer programs

   (b) play games with people from all around the world

   (c) Both of the above.

2. People can get to the World Wide Web through a _____ .

    (a) car   (b) computer (c) microwave

3. The Internet allows people all over the world to exchange information _____ .

    (a) slowly (b) quickly   (c) expensively

4. There are _____ files on the Internet than you could ever fit on your computer.

    (a) more   (b) less   (c) Cannot compare.

5. The files on the Internet are actually kept on the _____ of computers all around the world.

    (a) soft drives   (b) printers (c) hard drives

English Learning Strategy

I use flashcards to remember new English words.（我會使用單字卡來記憶英文生字。）

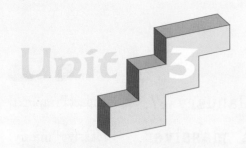

Unit 3

Earthquake in L.A.

At 4.31 in the morning on January 17, 1994, the full **impact**[1] of a **massive**[2] earthquake **measuring**[3] 6.7 on the Richter scale hit the community of Northridge in Los Angeles. It was an unwelcome wake-up call for everyone in the city.

One **resident**,[4] Rosemary Sato, was shaken awake in her bed to the sound of **tremors**[5] violently rocking her house. When she got up she found that the quake had blown open her front door and thrown her furniture around like toys.

However, the damage wasn't restricted to Northridge. Across the city the quake killed sixty people, destroyed or **severely**[6] damaged more than 3,000 homes, and brought down ten highway bridges. Many people were trapped under debris. The cost of the damage was **estimated**[7] to be $20 billion. The cause of this quake was movement in the San Andreas fault system. The fault is a **crack**[8]

impact [ˈɪmpækt]

massive [ˈmæsɪv]

measure [ˈmɛʒɚ]

resident [ˈrɛzədənt]

tremor [ˈtrɛmɚ]

severely [səˈvɪrlɪ]

estimate [ˈɛstəˌmet]

crack [kræk]

30

situated [ˈsɪtʃuˌetɪd]

between two giant pieces of the Earth's crust. One of these pieces, most of which is **situated**[9] under the Pacific Ocean, is moving at an average of about four centimetres every year.

prediction [prɪˈdɪkʃən]

The good news is that the Californian authorities are taking these **predictions**[10] seriously. Engineers are working to strengthen the steel frames of buildings and other structures such as bridges. Hopefully,

structural [ˈstrʌktʃərəl]

this will *lead to* less **structural**[11] damage during the next quake.

During a quake it is important to stay calm, as panic leads to rash actions which may *result in* injury or even death.

effect [əˈfɛkt, ɪˈfɛkt]

trauma [ˈtrɔmə]

Levon Jernazian, a clinical psychologist, helps people to *deal with* the **effects**[12] of this **trauma**.[13] For weeks after the Northridge quake, one of his patients, Ani Shakhverdyan, aged eight, would still *cling to* her parents, *was terrified of* the dark and would not even go to the bathroom alone.

Other survivors of quakes deal with their fears in a different way. They tell themselves that it won't happen again.

Little does she realise that in California, with the chances of another severe quake at 90 per cent in the next thirty years, she *is* very *likely* to **experience**[14] *at least* one more.

experience [ɪkˈspɪrɪəns]

In one session, Ani was asked to draw a picture of her fears. She drew a big rat. Then Levon Jernazian told her to cut the picture of the rat into pieces, burn it, and then jump on the **remains**.[15] Ani did what he suggested and her fears became less intense.

remains [rɪˈmenz]

Unfortunately, this movement isn't slow and continuous, but occurs in **bursts**,[16] which result in earthquakes. And to make matters worse, scientists not only expect more earthquakes in the near future, but also more powerful ones.

burst [bɝst]

People are advised to stay where they are and, if possible, to take **shelter**[17] under a bed or table. However, for many it is difficult to *get*

shelter [ˈʃɛltɚ]

rid of the terror of experiencing an earthquake. After the Northridge quake, thousands of Californians even left the state, and many of those who stayed have experienced what is now known as "earthquake trauma".

One woman's reaction was, "I'm not scared anymore. Also, it *'s similar to* being in a plane crash. What are your chances of being in another?"

Another resident of the community, who lived in a three-storey apartment block, recalls the top two floors of the building crashing down onto his first-floor apartment. "A wall fell on me," he said, "I couldn't move my head. I was **trapped**[18] for five hours with injuries to my lungs, ribs and **collar-bone**."[19]

Amazingly enough, nobody noticed it *apart from* scientists who were studying the seismic activity. However, one man did report that his dog had started to howl at the time the quake was said to have started.

The residents of California are also

trap [træp]

collar-bone [ˈkɑləˈbon]

preparing themselves for the next big one.
They are buying emergency supplies, *nailing
down* their **belongings**[20] and making plans for
what they should do *in the event of* another
quake.

90

belongings [bəˈlɔŋɪŋz]

A. **Vocabulary**

1. **impact** ['ɪmpækt] *n*. [C] the effect or influence that an event, situation, etc. has on someone or something 衝擊

   The President said he expected the meeting to have a marked *impact* on the future of the country.

2. **massive** ['mæsɪv] *adj*. very large in size, quantity, or extent 巨大的

   Sandy had a *massive* argument with her boyfriend last week.

3. **measure** ['mɛʒɚ] *vt*. to find the size, length, or amount of something using standard units 測量

   Could you please *measure* the length of the table for me?

4. **resident** ['rɛzədənt] *n*. [C] someone who lives or stays in a place such as a house or hotel 居住者

   The government should build more low cost homes for local *residents*.

5. **tremor** ['trɛmɚ] *n*. [C] a small earthquake 震動

   An earth *tremor* is a small earthquake in which the ground shakes slightly.

6. **severely** [sə'vɪrlɪ] *adv*. very badly or to a great degree 嚴重地

   Ken's movements are *severely* restricted.

7. **estimate** ['ɛstə,met] *vt*. to make a rough calculation 估計

   Try to *estimate* how many steps it will take to get to that window.

8. **crack** [kræk] *n*. [C] a very narrow space between two things or two parts of something 裂縫

   The children carefully avoided the *cracks* between the paving stones.

9. **situated** [ˈsɪtʃʊˌetɪd] *adj.* in a particular place or position 位於

This small town is *situated* just south of Cleveland.

10. **prediction** [prɪˈdɪkʃən] *n.* [C] something that you say is going to happen 預測

The old man was unwilling to make a *prediction* for the coming year.

11. **structural** [ˈstrʌktʃərəl] *adj.* connected with the structure of something 結構的

The explosion caused little *structural* damage to the office towers.

12. **effect** [əˈfɛkt, ɪˈfɛkt] *n.* [C] the result or consequence of an action etc. 影響

Parents sometimes worry about the *effect* of music on their children's behavior.

13. **trauma** [ˈtrɔmə] *n.* [U] a mental state of extreme shock caused by a very frightening or unpleasant experience （精神上的）創傷

The old lady had been through the *trauma* of losing her only son.

14. **experience** [ɪkˈspɪrɪəns] *vt.* to undergo; feel 經歷

These children had never *experienced* this kind of holiday before.

15. **remains** [rɪˈmenz] *n.* [C] （通常作 plural 用） the parts of something that are left after the rest has been destroyed or has disappeared 殘留物

The girls are tidying up the *remains* of their picnic.

16. **burst** [bɜst] *n.* [C] a sudden issue or outbreak 突發

It is easier to cope with short *bursts* of activity than with prolonged exercise.

17. **shelter** [ˈʃɛltɚ] *n.* [U] protection, from danger or from wind, rain, hot sun, etc. 遮蔽物

Those flowers grow well in the *shelter* of that big tree.

18. **trap** [træp] *vt.* to be in a bad situation from which you cannot escape 困住

The train was *trapped* underground by a fire.

19. **collar-bone** [ˈkɑlɚˌbon] *n.* [C] the bone joining the breast-bone and shoulder-blade 鎖骨

Jackson had a broken *collar-bone*.

20. **belongings** [bə'lɔŋɪŋz] *n.* [C]（通常作 plural 用） the things that you own, especially those that you can carry with you　攜帶物品；所有物

Please ensure that you have all your *belongings* when you leave the hotel.

B. Idioms & Phrases

1. **lead to** to make something happen or exist as a result　導致

   That investment program will *lead to* the creation of hundreds of new jobs.

2. **result in** to have a specified end or outcome　致使

   That accident *resulted in* the death of two passengers.

3. **deal with** to succeed in controlling an emotional problem so that it does not affect your life　處理

   She saw a psychiatrist who helped her *deal with* her fear.

4. **cling to** to stick to someone or something or seem to surround them　抱住

   She had to *cling to* the door handle until the pain passed.

5. **be terrified of** very frightened　被…驚嚇

   Mary *is terrified of* heights.

6. **be likely** probable; such as may well happen or be true　大概

   If this is your first baby, it *is* far more *likely* that you'll get to the hospital too early.

7. **at least** not less than　至少

   It will take the girl *at least* 20 minutes to get there.

8. **get rid of** to take action so that you no longer have something unpleasant that you do not want　除去

   I can't *get rid of* this cough.

9. **be similar to** almost the same but not exactly the same　與…相似

Kevin's opinion on the matter *is similar to* mine.

10. **apart from** except for　除…之外

Apart from the vegetables, what did you buy for our dinner?

11. **nail down** to hold fast; keep fixed　使固定

We'll have to *nail* all the stuff *down* by ten o'clock.

12. **in the event of** if something happens　如果

The U.K. agreed to support the U.S. *in the event of* war.

C. Word Forms

1. **adj. + -ly → adv.**

violent（強烈的）	→	violently（強烈地）
severe（劇烈的）	→	severely（劇烈地）
serious（嚴重的）	→	seriously（嚴重地）
unfortunate（不幸的）	→	unfortunately（不幸地）
amazing（令人驚奇的）	→	amazingly（令人驚奇地）

Barbara has been acting very ***strangely*** lately. I wonder if anything is wrong.

Perhaps I should ask her about her ***strange*** behavior.

2. **n. + -ful → adj.**

hope（希望）	→	hopeful（懷希望的）
power（力量）	→	powerful（有力的）

I was in great *pain* when I knew she passed away.

The news was *painful* to me.

1. You cannot express your point of view _____ (adequate) in only 100 words.

2. Many people believe that murder is an _____ (extreme) serious crime, and that murderers deserve capital punishment.

3. This will be _____ (help) to you when you are grown up.

D. Sentence Patterns

1. not only...but (also) （不僅…而且）

Scientists *not only* expect more earthquakes in the near future, *but also* more powerful ones.

(1) Shirley is *not only* attractive *but (also)* intelligent.

(2) Joe *not only* smokes *but (also)* drinks.

2. Little + Aux. + S. + V.P. （根本不）

little 置於 know, think, care, suspect, realize, dream 等動詞之前。 (= not at all)

 Little does she realise that in California, with the chances of another severe quake at 90 per cent in the next thirty years, she is very likely to experience at least one more.

(1) *Little did* he dream a letter from his father.

(2) *Little does* she know that she has failed the exam.

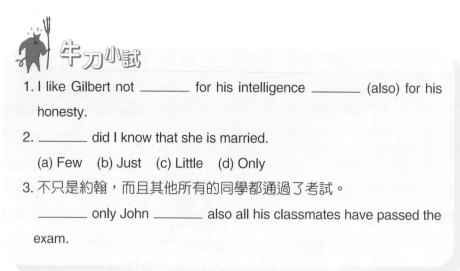

牛刀小試

1. I like Gilbert not _____ for his intelligence _____ (also) for his honesty.

2. _____ did I know that she is married.

  (a) Few (b) Just (c) Little (d) Only

3. 不只是約翰，而且其他所有的同學都通過了考試。

  _____ only John _____ also all his classmates have passed the exam.

E. Exercise

I. True/False: *Decide true (T) or false (F) of the following statements based on the text.*

❶ On January 17, 1994, the damage of a massive earthquake wasn't restricted to Northridge.

❷ The Californian authorities are not taking these predictions seriously.

❸ It is important to stay calm during a quake.

❹ There are few chances of another severe quake in California in the next thirty years.

❺ People are advised to stay where they are when an earthquake happens.

II. Vocabulary Review: *Complete the sentences with the following words of appropriate forms.*

furniture	shelter	average	prediction	calm
severely	panic	realize	expect	experience

❶ The small house provided a _____ from the storm.

❷ I've never _____ the pleasure of winning the beauty contest before.

❸ We had little _____ for our new house.

❹ The students got into a _____ when the teacher said he decided to fail half of the students.

❺ The weather _____ said tomorrow will be a rainy day.

❻ The scenery was not so fine as we _____ .

❼ You will _____ how hard the work is.

❽ They made a loss today, but on _____ they make a profit.

❾ The new laws are _____ enforced.

❿ A deep _____ filled the room.

III. Multiple Choice: *Choose the most appropriate word based on the meaning of the context.*

❶ This book deals _____ economics.

    (a) with   (b) on   (c) for   (d) about

❷ She is terrified _____ being scolded about it.

    (a) at   (b) in   (c) of   (d) by

❸ Tom is asked to get rid _____ his bad behaviors.

    (a) by   (b) to   (c) of   (d) with

❹ My new car is similar _____ John's.

    (a) as   (b) from   (c) in   (d) to

❺ Apart _____ your sister, who will be there?

    (a) from   (b) or   (c) for   (d) with

IV. Cloze Test: *Fill in the blanks with the most appropriate words based on the meaning of the context.*

Levon Jernazian, a clinical psychologist, helps people to ^{1}_____ with the effects of this trauma. For weeks after the Northridge quake, one of his ^{2}_____ , Ani Shakhverdyan, aged eight, would still cling to her parents, was terrified of the dark and would not even go to the bathroom ^{3}_____ . In one session, Ani was asked to ^{4}_____ a picture of her fears. She drew a big rat. Then Levon Jernazian told her to cut the picture of the ^{5}_____ into pieces, burn it, and then jump on the remains. Ani did ^{6}_____ he suggested and her fears became ^{7}_____ intense.

V. Translation: *Translate the following Chinese sentences into English.*

❶ 當她起床時，她發現地震已震開她的前門，而且她的傢俱也像玩具一樣被晃到四處。

_____

❷ 損失金額估計達 200 億。

_____

❸ 地震發生時，保持鎮定是很重要的。

_____

❹ 地震後的其他生還者，用不同的方法去處理他們的恐懼感。

_____

❺ 然而對很多人來說，要擺脫經歷地震的恐懼感是很困難的。

_____

VI. Discussion Topics: *Discuss the following topics on "earthquake" in oral or written reports.*

❶ Please describe the massive earthquake which occurred in Taiwan on September 21, 1999.

❷ How do you deal with your fears of the 921 earthquake?

❸ What will you plan to do in the event of another earthquake?

Outside Reading

Tornadoes

Tornadoes are storms with very strong turning winds and dark clouds. These winds are perhaps the strongest on earth. They reach speeds of 300 miles per hour. The dark clouds are shaped like a funnel—wide at the top and narrow at the bottom. The winds are strongest in the center of the funnel.

Tornadoes are especially common in the United States, but only in certain parts. They occur mainly in the central states.

A hot afternoon in the spring is the most likely time for a tornado. Clouds become dark. There is thunder, lightning, and rain. A cloud forms a funnel and begins to twist. The funnel moves faster and faster. The faster the winds, the louder the noise. Tornadoes always move in a northeastern direction. They never last longer than eight hours.

A tornado's path is narrow, but within that narrow path a tornado can destroy everything. It can smash buildings and rip up trees. Tornadoes can kill people as well.

The worst tornado swept through the states of Missouri, Illinois, and Indiana in 1925, killing 689 people. Modern weather equipment now makes it possible to warn people of tornadoes. People have a much better chance of protecting themselves. But nothing can stop tornadoes from destroying everything in their path.

Reading Comprehension

1. With regard to tornadoes, the winds are strongest _____ of the funnel.

   (a) at the top   (b) in the center   (c) at the bottom

2. Tornadoes are especially common in the United States. They occur mainly in the _____ states.

   (a) central (b) southern   (c) eastern

3. Tornadoes always move in a _____ direction.

   (a) northwestern   (b) southeastern   (c) northeastern

4. A hot afternoon in the _____ is the most likely time for a tornado.

   (a) spring   (b) summer   (c) fall

5. Tornadoes never last longer than _____ hours.

   (a) two   (b) four   (c) eight

English Learning Strategy

I watch TV shows or movies spoken in English.（我會觀賞英語發音的電視節目或電影。）

Unit 4

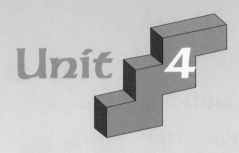

Thanksgiving Days

When the first Europeans **settled**[1] in America they arrived too late to **sow**[2] **crops**[3] for the following year's **harvest**.[4] Nearly half the settlers *died of* **starvation**[5] during that first winter. The next spring, those who had **survived**[6] *were able to* plant their seeds and, after an excellent summer harvest, they celebrated with a **festival**.[7] The festival *became known as* Thanksgiving Day, and in 1941 it was given the **fixed**[8] date each year of the fourth Thursday in November.

Food is an important part of Thanksgiving **celebrations**.[9] Traditional thanksgiving foods include turkey, which is eaten with cranberry **sauce**,[10] and pumpkin pie. At Thanksgiving, as many of the family as possible will gather together. Like many other public holidays, Thanksgiving is often celebrated with street parties and sporting events.

Thanksgiving is also celebrated in Canada, where it is held on the second Monday in October. Canadians hold Thanksgiving before

settle ['sɛtl̩]

sow [so]

crop [krɑp]

harvest ['hɑrvɪst]

starvation [stɑr'veʃən]

survive [sɚ'vaɪv]

festival ['fɛstəvl̩]

fixed [fɪkst]

celebration
  [ˌsɛlə'breʃən]

sauce [sɔs]

48

the Americans because winter begins earlier in Canada than the USA. 25

In Japan, one of the most important harvests is that of the autumn rice crop. Traditionally, none of the newly-grown rice could be eaten until a 30 **ceremony**[11] had been held to **honour**[12] the **spirits**[13] which were thought to protect the rice while it grew. There was a **procession**[14] and a great **banquet**,[15] at which 35 ceremonial dances were performed. At midnight, the Emperor of Japan *took part in* a ritual, presenting a portion of the harvest at a **sacred**[16] **altar**.[17] Today the festival is a public holiday, when people celebrate the success of 40 Japanese industry and farming. It is called Labour Thanksgiving Day.

ceremony [ˈsɛrəˌmonɪ]

honour [ˈɑnɚ]

spirit [ˈspɪrɪt]

procession [prəˈsɛʃən]

banquet [ˈbæŋkwɪt]

sacred [ˈsekrɪd]

altar [ˈɔltɚ]

A. Vocabulary

1. **settle** [ˈsɛtl] *vi.* to go to live in a new place, and stay there 定居

   After returning from Brazil, the old lady *settled* in Chicago.

2. **sow** [so] *vt.* to plant or scatter seeds on a piece of ground 播種

   Farmers *sow* the seed in a warm place in March.

3. **crop** [krɑp] *n.* [C] a plant such as wheat, rice, or fruit that is grown by farmers, especially in order to be eaten 農作物；穀類

   Most of the land in this area is used for growing *crops*.

4. **harvest** [ˈhɑrvɪst] *n.* [U] process of gathering in crops etc. 收割

   There was about 300 million tons of grain in the field at the start of the *harvest*.

5. **starvation** [stɑrˈveʃən] *n.* [U] suffering or death caused by lack of food 飢餓

   Over three hundred people have died of *starvation* since the beginning of the year.

6. **survive** [səˈvaɪv] *vi.* to continue to live or exist 生還，存活

   Only one passenger *survived* in this accident.

7. **festival** [ˈfɛstəvl] *n.* [C] a day or period of celebration 節日

   Easter is a Christian *festival*.

8. **fixed** [fɪkst] *adj.* staying the same and not varying 固定的

   The wholesaler sold the products to its customers with *fixed* prices.

9. **celebration** [ˌsɛləˈbreʃən] *n.* [C] an occasion or party when you celebrate

something 慶典

There will be a *celebration* in Candy's house tomorrow night.

10. **sauce** [sɔs] *n.* [U] a thick cooked liquid that is served with food to give it a particular taste 醬汁

I would like to have some vanilla ice cream with chocolate *sauce*.

11. **ceremony** [ˈsɛrəˌmonɪ] *n.* [C] a formal procedure, especially at a public event or anniversary 儀式

The award *ceremony* will take place in the school tomorrow morning.

12. **honour** [ˈɑnɚ] *vt.* to treat or regard someone with special attention and respect 尊敬

Mr. Reddy was *honoured* by being made a knight of St. Gregory.

13. **spirit** [ˈspɪrɪt] *n.* [C] the part of someone that is believed to continue to live after they have died 神靈

Although Larry is dead, I can feel his *spirit* with me.

14. **procession** [prəˈsɛʃən] *n.* [C] a line of people or vehicles moving slowly as part of a ceremony 遊行

There is a funeral *procession* on the street.

15. **banquet** [ˈbæŋkwɪt] *n.* [C] a grand formal dinner 宴會

Tom attended a state *banquet* last night.

16. **sacred** [ˈsekrɪd] *adj.* connected with a god or religion 神聖的

The owl is *sacred* for many Californian Indian people.

17. **altar** [ˈɔltɚ] *n.* [C] a table or flat block for sacrifice or offering to a deity 祭壇

Those children blew out the candles on the *altar*.

 **. Idioms & Phrases**

1. **die of** to stop living and become dead 死於（疾病或飢餓）
   Both that little girl and her mother *died of* starvation in the snow.

2. **be able to** to have the capacity or power 能夠
   The older child should *be able to* prepare a simple meal.

3. **become known as** someone or something that is clearly
   recognized by or familiar to all people 著名的
   Mozart *became known as* a famous musician when he was
   only four years old.

4. **take part in** to do something together with other people 參加
   Thousands of students are *taking part in* the demonstration.

 **. Word Forms**

1. $\boxed{\textbf{v.} + \begin{cases} \textbf{-ant} \\ \textbf{-ent} \end{cases} \rightarrow \textbf{adj.}}$

    excel（勝過）   →   excellent（極好的）

    import（重要） →   important（重要的）

 Jane *assisted* the manager in his work.

   Jane was an *assistant* secretary.

2. $\boxed{\textbf{v.} + \textbf{-ion} \rightarrow \textbf{n.}}$

celebrate（慶祝）	→	celebration（慶祝）
process（列隊前進）	→	procession（列隊進行）

 I have not **decided** yet where to apply to graduate school.

I need to make some other important **decision** first, such as whether to stay in this country or go back home.

1. The two coats are _____ (differ) in size and material.
2. Barbara made several wonderful _____ (suggest) at the meeting last week.
3. The baby saw her _____ (reflect) in the mirror and smiled.

D. Sentence Patterns

1. too...to（太…以致不能）

 When the first Europeans settled in America they arrived **too** late **to** sow crops for the following year's harvest.

(1) Mark is **too** short **to** touch the ceiling.

(2) Jessie was **too** tired **to** walk any farther.

2. as + ... + as possible（儘可能）

 At Thanksgiving, **as** many of the family **as possible** will gather together.

(1) You should get up **as** early **as possible** tomorrow morning.

(2) Tom told me about the accident in **as** much detail **as possible**.

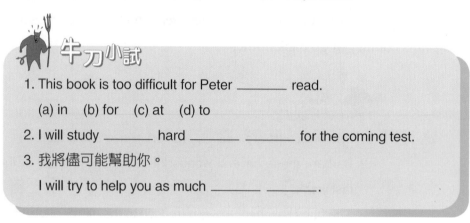

牛刀小試

1. This book is too difficult for Peter _____ read.

   (a) in   (b) for   (c) at   (d) to

2. I will study _____ hard _____ _____ for the coming test.

3. 我將儘可能幫助你。

   I will try to help you as much _____ _____.

. Exercise

I. True/False: *Decide true (T) or false (F) of the following statements based on the text.*

❶ The first European settlers in America arrived in time to sow crops for the following year's harvest.

❷ Thanksgiving was given the fixed date each year of the fourth Thursday in November.

❸ Traditional thanksgiving foods include turkey and apple pie.

❹ Canadians hold Thanksgiving after the Americans.

❺ Japanese celebrate the success of industry and farming on Labor Thanksgiving Day.

II. Vocabulary Review: *Complete the sentences with the following words of appropriate forms.*

starvation	seed	include	protect	banquet
sauce	public	survive	become	harvest

❶ They made a _____ protest against it.

❷ This price _____ service charges and tips.

❸ The young couple decided to hold a wedding _____ .

❹ Even nowadays many people in Africa die of _____ .

❺ The old farmer had a rich _____ last year.

❻ Jack _____ an operation.

❼ She has _____ a famous woman.

❽ Farmers sow _____ in Spring.

❾ May God _____ you.

❿ Two _____ are served with the meat course.

III. Multiple Choice: *Choose the most appropriate word based on the meaning of the context.*

❶ Professor Smith promised to take part _____ the meeting.

   (a) in   (b) at   (c) on   (d) to

❷ My sister is able _____ play flute very well.

   (a) in   (b) for   (c) with   (d) to

❸ Jean became known _____ a good writer after she published her second novel.

   (a) for   (b) as   (c) about   (d) in

❹ Kevin's mother died _____ lung cancer.

   (a) as   (b) in   (c) of   (d) about

❺ Carlotta's father is a good cook. He is _____ to cook delicious food.

   (a) about   (b) able   (c) around   (d) try

IV. Cloze Test: *Fill in the blanks with the most appropriate words based on the meaning of the context.*

Food is an important part of ^{1}_____ celebrations. Traditional thanksgiving ^{2}_____ include turkey, which is ^{3}_____ with cranberry sauce, and pumpkin ^{4}_____ . At Thanksgiving, as many of the family as ^{5}_____ will gather together. Like many ^{6}_____ public holidays, Thanksgiving is often ^{7}_____ with street parties and sporting events.

V. Translation: *Translate the following Chinese sentences into English.*

❶ 在第一個冬天裡，將近一半的移民死於飢餓。

_____

❷ 食物是感恩節的慶祝儀式中重要的一部份。

_____

❸ 感恩節通常以街道遊行及體育活動的方式來慶祝。

_____

❹ 加拿大的冬天比美國的冬天來得早。

_____

❺ 在午夜的時候，日皇在聖壇上獻上一部份的收穫物。

_____

VI. Discussion Topics: *Discuss the following topics on "holiday" in oral or written reports.*

❶ Please compare the customs of Thanksgiving, Christmas, and Halloween.

❷ Is there a similar holiday like Thanksgiving in Taiwan? If yes, please describe it.

❸ Which Chinese holiday do you like most? Why?

Outside Reading

Who Really Discovered America?

For a long time, people believed that Christopher Columbus was the first person from Europe to land in the New World. But recent findings have shown that several other people may have journeyed to America long before Columbus.

One group of explorers who probably beat Columbus to America was the Vikings. They came from Northern Europe to Iceland and Greenland. They may have made voyages as far west as Canada more than 800 years ago. The Vikings did not leave any records. But Eskimo carvings made more than 800 years ago show people dressed the way the Vikings did.

The Vikings may not have been the first to come to America either. St. Brendan, an Irish monk, may have landed in Canada more than 1,200 years ago. Old writings show that the monk left Ireland in a leather boat. He had a small crew with him. Several years ago, a modern explorer sailed the same kind of boat from Ireland to Canada in 50 days. St. Brendan may have made the same trip. No one knows for sure.

Columbus may not have been first. He is the most important explorer, however. Why? Soon after Columbus' four trips, other explorers came to the New World. They decided to settle here. They set up new homes on American soil.

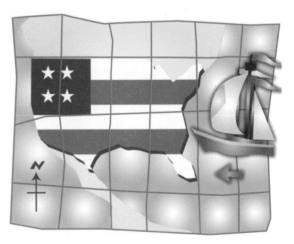

Reading Comprehension

1. Recent findings have shown that _____ people may have traveled to America long before Columbus.

    (a) no other   (b) several other   (c) a lot of

2. _____ may have landed in Canada more than 1,200 years ago.

    (a) Columbus   (b) The Vikings   (c) St. Brendan

3. The Vikings came from _____ Europe.

    (a) Southern   (b) Northern   (c) Western

4. _____ is the most important explorer of America.

    (a) Columbus   (b) The Vikings   (c) St. Brendan

5. Columbus has journeyed to America _____ .

    (a) once   (b) two times   (c) four times

English Learning Strategy

I first skim an English passage (read over the passage quickly); then go back and read carefully.（閱讀英文段落時，我會先瀏覽一遍，然後再回頭精讀。）

Unit 5

Fictional Heroes Never Die

James Bond (1953–　)

Bugs Bunny (1937–　)

Batman (1939–　)

Charlie Brown (1950–　)

Kermit (1957–　)

Real **heroes**[1] are only human. They live and die like the **rest**[2] of us. But **fictional**[3] heroes are different. They began life many years ago and they will *live on* in fiction in the future. Here are some favorite twentieth-century fictional heroes.

1 The **spy**[4] 007 has been working for the British Secret Service since 1953 when Ian Fleming first wrote about him in *Casino Royale*. Fleming is now dead, but the spy still lives on. The first movie was *Dr. No* in 1962 and since then he's appeared in *more than* twenty movies. The Cold War has finished and Bond's **enemies**[5] are not the Russians now, but there are still *plenty of* bad people out there! Columbia, the movie company, recently finished **filming**[6] his latest **adventure**.[7]

2 He first saved Gotham City from evil, with the help of Robin, in a **comic**[8] book in 1939 and has been **fighting**[9] crime for more than fifty years. The team has made three TV series, *as well as* movies and novels. The most popular

hero [ˈhɪro]

rest [rɛst]

fictional [ˈfɪkʃən!]

spy [spaɪ]

enemy [ˈɛnəmɪ]

film [fɪlm]

adventure [ədˈvɛntʃɚ]

comic [ˈkɑmɪk]

fight [faɪt]

TV series was in the 1960s, and our hero has recently appeared in movies. He will live on *as long as* there are **criminals**[10] like the Penguin, Catwoman, and the Joker in Gotham City.

criminal ['krɪmənl]

25

3 He has been *living with* his pet dog Snoopy in a small American town since 1950, when he first appeared in the cartoon **strip**[11] *Peanuts.* More than forty years later, he still experiences all the happiness and **frustration**[12] of a **typical**[13] boy, playing baseball with his friends and going to school. His first appearance on television was in 1965 and *so far* he has made three big-screen movies. His appeal is as strong as ever.

strip [strɪp]

frustration [frʌsˈtreʃən]

typical [ˈtɪpɪkl]

30

35

4 The talking rabbit first asked "What's Up Doc?" in 1937 and has been eating carrots *in public ever since.* He has appeared in comic books, newspaper **cartoons**,[14] and *above all, hundreds of* movies. He will be popular for as long as people *laugh at* rabbits.

cartoon [karˈtun]

40

5 The green frog has been singing and dancing on television since 1957, although it

45 was only in 1967 that he became famous with the Muppets. Since then, 235 million people in one hundred countries have seen hundreds of Muppet shows. There have also been three movies. Success has not changed him; he

50 **remains**[15] **exactly**[16] the same color.

remain [rɪˈmen]

exactly [ɪgˈzæktlɪ]

A . Vocabulary

1. **hero** [ˈhɪro] *n.* [C] a person noted or admired for nobility, courage, outstanding achievements, etc.　英雄

   People think you are some sort of *hero*.

2. **rest** [rɛst] *n.* [U] all the parts of something or all the things in a group that remain 其他；剩餘

   Bob will be in a wheelchair for the *rest* of his life.

3. **fictional** [ˈfɪkʃənl] *adj.* imaginary　虛構的

   Everyone knows that Superman is a *fictional* hero.

4. **spy** [spaɪ] *n.* [C] a person who secretly collects and reports information for a government, company, etc.　間諜

   James Bond is a British *spy* in the movies of 007.

5. **enemy** [ˈɛnəmɪ] *n.* [C] someone who opposes you and wants to prevent you from doing something　敵人

   That presidential candidate has many political *enemies*.

6. **film** [fɪlm] *vt.* to use a camera to record a story or real events so that it can be shown in the cinema or on TV　拍攝

   The movie company has *filmed* her life story.

7. **adventure** [ədˈvɛntʃɚ] *n.* [C] an unusual and exciting experience　冒險

   The young man is talking about his *adventures* at sea.

8. **comic** [ˈkɑmɪk] *adj.* of drawings telling a story　漫畫的

   Jane loved to read Japanese *comic* books.

9. **fight** [faɪt] *vt.* to try in a determined way to prevent something unpleasant or stop it happening　對抗

Mother Teresa devoted her life to *fighting* poverty.

10. **criminal** [ˈkrɪmənḷ] *n.* [C] a person guilty of a crime　罪犯

How could the people elect the *criminal* to office?

11. **strip** [strɪp] *n.* [C] a series of drawings which tell a story in a newspaper or magazine　連載（漫畫）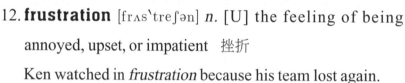

Some children like to read comic *strips* in magazines.

12. **frustration** [frʌˈtreʃən] *n.* [U] the feeling of being annoyed, upset, or impatient　挫折

Ken watched in *frustration* because his team lost again.

13. **typical** [ˈtɪpɪkḷ] *adj.* having the usual features or qualities of a particular group or thing　典型的

This article is *typical* of her early work.

14. **cartoon** [kɑrˈtun] *n.* [C] a funny drawing in a newspaper, often including humorous remarks about news events　漫畫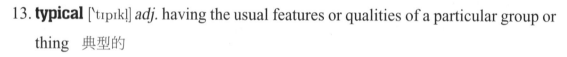

Both adults and children love this funny *cartoon*.

15. **remain** [rɪˈmen] *vi.* to be in the same place or condition during further time　依然是…

The political leader *remained* in power for ten years.

16. **exactly** [ɪgˈzæktlɪ] *adv.* precisely　完全地

The twin sisters are wearing *exactly* the same clothes.

B . Idioms & Phrases

1. **live on** to continue to exist 活下去

   Daniel's life has been cut short by this terrible virus but his younger sister will *live on* after him.

2. **more than** greater than the actual number or amount 超過

   This new house costs *more than* ten million NT dollars.

3. **plenty of** sufficient quantity or number 很多的

   There is still *plenty of* time to go out for dinner.

4. **as well as** in addition to something else 不僅；除⋯外

   That kind man gave me clothes *as well as* food.

5. **as long as** provided that 只要

   You can go out to play *as long as* you finish your homework.

6. **live with** to live together 與⋯同居

   The old couple has one daughter who still *lives with* them.

7. **so far** until now 到目前為止

   Everything is going well *so far*.

8. **in public** doing something where everyone can see 公開地

   Jean's husband is always nice to her *in public*.

9. **ever since** for the whole of a long period of time after a particular time or event in the past 從⋯時起

   Her parents came to the UK in 1982 and have lived there *ever since*.

10. **above all** most of all; more than anything else 最重要的是

    Ariel is kind, hardworking, and *above all* honest.

11. **hundreds of** a lot of things or people 很多的

Today you can buy *hundreds of* flavors of ice cream.

12. **laugh at** to make fun of 嘲笑

Cindy thinks people *laugh at* her because she is ugly.

C . Word Forms

1. adj. + -ness → n.

happy（快樂的）　→　happiness（快樂）

 My granddaughters are very **happy** children.

Their **happiness** is important to my son.

2. v. + -ance → n.

appear（出現）　→　appearance（出現）

 John **appears** to be very unhappy.

His sad **appearance** makes his friends wonder what's wrong.

 牛刀小試

1. Daniel is looking forward to my first _____ (perform) tonight.

2. My uncle overcome his _____ (lonely) by going out more often with his friends.

3. The _____ (shy) often prevents students from doing well in school.

D. Sentence Patterns

1. $S_1 + \begin{cases} 現在完成式 \\ 現在完成進行式 \end{cases} + since + S_2 + 過去式（自從，自⋯以來）$

EX The spy 007 has been working for the British Secret Service *since* 1953.
He has been living with his pet dog Snoopy in a small American town *since* 1950.

(1) They have been learning Chinese *since* they came to Taiwan.

(2) Tom has studied English for two years *since* he was seven years old.

2. NP_1 + as well as + NP_2（⋯也同樣地；不但⋯而且）

EX The team has made three TV series, *as well as* movies and novels.

(1) I gave Tom a pencil *as well as* an eraser.

(2) John *as well as* you is very tall.

 牛刀小試

1. I have been living in this small town _____ I was six years old.

   (a) when (b) since (c) while (d) as

2. She has experience _____ _____ _____ knowledge.

3. 傑克與他的朋友一起在那次車禍中受傷。

   Jack, as well _____ his friends, was injured in the accident.

E . Exercise

I. Match: *Match the names with the following statements.*

(A) Kermit (B) Bugs Bunny (C) James Bond (D) Batman (E) Charlie Brown

❶ The spy 007 has been working for the British Secret Service since 1953.

❷ He first saved Gotham City from evil, with the help of Robin, in a comic book in 1939.

❸ He has been living with his pet dog Snoopy in a small American town since 1950.

❹ The talking rabbit first asked "What's Up Doc?" in 1937.

❺ The green frog has been singing and dancing on television since 1957.

II. Vocabulary Review: *Complete the sentences with the following words of appropriate forms.*

typical	criminal	frustration	strip	fictional
exactly	fight	hero	enemy	remain

❶ Any father can be a _____ to his son.

❷ Its internal unity was in large measure _____ .

❸ *The China Post* usually has comic _____ on the first page on Sundays.

❹ Elizabeth has deep _____ in English.

❺ Children with emotional difficulties sometimes _____ in school.

❻ Some people believe that one's biggest _____ is oneself.

❼ The natural beauty of that country _____ unchanged.

❽ Everybody is innocent before he is proven to be a _____ .

❾ It is _____ of him to bring nothing to a party.

❿ Please repeat _____ what he said.

III. Multiple Choice: *Choose the most appropriate word based on the meaning of the context.*

❶ There were plenty _____ good places to camp in.

(a) at　　　　(b) of　　　　(c) in　　　　(d) to

❷ He has experience as _____ as knowledge.

(a) willing　　(b) will　　　(c) long　　　(d) well

❸ Frank insulted me _____ public.

(a) in　　　　(b) on　　　　(c) at　　　　(d) under

❹ Living _____ Steve is not easy.

(a) in　　　　(b) of　　　　(c) to　　　　(d) with

❺ _____ of people came to the concert.

(a) A hundred　(b) Hundreds　(c) Hundred　(d) Two hundreds

IV. Cloze Test: *Fill in the blanks with the most appropriate words based on the meaning of the context.*

He and Robbin has ¹_____ fighting crime for more ²_____ fifty years. The team has made three TV series, as ³_____ as movies and novels. The most popular TV ⁴_____ was in the 1960s, and our hero ⁵_____ recently appeared in movies! He will live ⁶_____ as long as there are criminals ⁷_____ the Penguin, Catwoman, and the Joker in Gotham City.

V. Translation: *Translate the following Chinese sentences into English.*

❶ 真實的英雄跟我們其他人一樣生存和死亡。

_____

❷ 冷戰已經結束，龐德的敵人現在不是俄國人了。

_____

❸ 他於 1965 年第一次出現在電視上，至今他已演過 3 部大銀幕電影。

_____

❹ 他將會受人歡迎，只要人們看到兔寶寶會笑。

_____

❺ 成功並沒有改變他，他仍保持完全相同的顏色。

VI. Discussion Topics: *Discuss the following topics on "fictional hero" in oral or written reports.*

❶ Are you familiar with any of the five fictional heroes in the text? If yes, please tell his story to the class.

❷ Can you think of any Chinese fictional hero? If yes, make a short description of him.

❸ Which fictional hero do you admire most? Why?

Outside Reading

The Beatles

When John Lennon was murdered outside his New York apartment by a young man for whom he had earlier autographed a record sleeve, it signalled the end of an era. The faint hope that one day the Beatles might get together again had gone for ever.

The Beatles: George Harrison, John Lennon, Paul McCartney and Ringo Starr, were formed in Liverpool in 1960. Harrison, Lennon and McCartney had gained experience playing at a club in Hamburg, but it was at the 'Cavern', in Liverpool, their home city, that the Beatles' career really began to take off.

Their first record, 'Love me do', was issued in October, 1962. Four months later their second, 'Please, please me', went straight into the top ten and soon reached the coveted number one spot, while their first L.P. became the fastest-selling L.P. of 1963. Although the group broke up, millionaires all, years ago, their records still sell all over the world. What is it that made the Beatles special?

As a group they were competent and their voices were pleasant, but this would not have been enough. They were probably lucky in their influences: the rich Merseyside environment from which they sprang, combined with an admiration for black American rhythm-and-blues; and they were fortunate in the rapport that they found with one another and with their audience, while the songwriting partnership of Lennon and McCartney produced a stream of brilliant hits.

Their themes were precisely those that occupied and concerned their young audience: love, sorrow, good luck, bad luck and the quaint characters that are always to be found in any big city. In addition they created melodies that were rich and original enough to be played and sung by musicians of the calibre of Count Basie and Ella Fitzgerald.

The Beatles were special because they believed in their own talents. They copied no-one, and they were strong enough not to allow themselves to be destroyed by the overnight achievement of success beyond the reach of the imagination. In this they probably owed much to their record producer George Martin and their manager Brian Epstein.

Reading Comprehension

1. John Lennon died from _____ .

   (a) accident   (b) murder   (c) suicide

2. The Beatles' career really started to become successful in _____ .

   (a) Hamburg   (b) Liverpool   (c) New York

3. The songwriting partnership in the Beatles included _____ .

   (a) Lennon and McCartney

   (b) Starr and Harrison

   (c) Lennon and Harrison

4. The Beatles enjoyed listening to _____ .

   (a) rock-and-roll   (b) country music   (c) rhythm-and blues

5. According to the author, the Beatles were special because _____ .

   (a) their voices were pleasant

   (b) they were lucky in their influences

   (c) they believed in their own talents

English Learning Strategy

I look for words in my own language that are similar to new words in English. （我會尋找與英文生字意義類似的中文字。）

Unit 6

Christmas Traditions

The ways of celebrating Christmas have changed little since it replaced Saturnalia. From Saturnalia came the traditions of **feasting**,[1] giving parties and

5 **decorating**[2] homes with evergreen plants *such as* holly and **ivy**[3]—a **reminder**[4] that even at midwinter the powers of nature survived. When Christianity came to northern

holly

10 Europe, the **missionaries**[5] found that the Celts and other local tribes also honoured the evergreens at the winter **solstice**.[6] **Mistletoe**[7] was a sacred plant to the Druids of Britain and, although it was never used as an official

15 part of Christian celebrations, at Christmas many British people still pin a **sprig**[8] of mistletoe over a fireplace or at the **entrance**[9] to the home.

Other Christmas customs have *come from*

20 northern Europe. Some ancient peoples believed that at the winter solstice the god Odin visited earth to **reward**[10] good and

feast [fist]

decorate [ˈdɛkəˌret]

ivy [ˈaɪvɪ]

reminder [rɪˈmaɪndəʳ]

missionary [ˈmɪʃənˌɛrɪ]

solstice [ˈsɑlstɪs]

mistletoe [ˈmɪslˌto]

sprig [sprɪg]

entrance [ˈɛntrəns]

reward [rɪˈwɔrd]

punish [ˈpʌnɪʃ]

evil [ˈivl̩]

legend [ˈlɛdʒənd]

welcome [ˈwɛlkəm]

parade [pəˈred]

march [mɑrtʃ]

punish[11] evil.[12] As Christianity spread, St Nicholas replaced Odin in the solstice legends,[13] bringing gifts at Christmas to good 25 children. In the Netherlands there is still a festival of St Nicholas on 6 December. The name Santa Claus has *developed from* the Dutch name for St Nicholas— Sinterklaas. 30

At Christmas, families come together to eat on Christmas Day. Many Christians go to church on Christmas Eve for a special ceremony at midnight to welcome[14] the day when Christ was born. 35 Relatives and friends give presents, and on Christmas morning, children wake eagerly to see if Santa Claus has left them a special gift.

In countries with warm climates, Christmas is also a time for public 40 celebrations. In Australia there are huge parades[15] with marching[16] bands. In Bombay and Goa in India there are midnight services held outdoors.

 A . Vocabulary

1. **feast** [fist] *vi.* to eat and drink a lot to celebrate something　宴會

   On the day when I get married, I'll *feast* in that big restaurant.

2. **decorate** ['dɛkə,ret] *vt.* to make something look more attractive by putting something pretty on it　裝飾

   He *decorates* his new room with big pictures and posters.

3. **ivy** ['aɪvɪ] *n.* [U] a climbing plant with dark green shiny leaves　常春藤

   That wall covered with *ivy* drew my attention.

4. **reminder** [rɪ'maɪndɚ] *n.* [C] a thing that reminds　提醒物

   In the car Hans saw a *reminder* of the dangers of drinking and driving.

5. **missionary** ['mɪʃən,ɛrɪ] *n.* [C] a person working for the church　傳教士

   He spent 30 years in Africa as a *missionary*.

6. **solstice** ['sɑlstɪs] *n.* [C] the time of either the longest or the shortest day of the year　至日

   The summer *solstice* and the winter *solstice* are the two times of the year when the sun is farthest away from the equator.

7. **mistletoe** ['mɪsl̩,to] *n.* [U] a plant with small white berries which grows over other trees, and is often used as decoration at Christmas　槲寄生（裝飾聖誕樹用）

   Mistletoe is used in Britain as a Christmas decoration.

8. **sprig** [sprɪg] *n.* [C] a small stem or part of a branch with leaves or flowers on it

小樹枝

That strange young man always brings a *sprig* of parsley with him.

9. **entrance** ['ɛntrəns] *n.* [C] a place for entering 入口

Amy's mother is waiting for her at the front *entrance* of the school.

10. **reward** [rɪ'wɔrd] *vt.* to give something to someone because they have done something good or helpful 獎賞

I'll *reward* your kindness by doing everything that helps you.

11. **punish** ['pʌnɪʃ] *vt.* to make someone suffer because they have done something wrong or broken the law 懲罰

The little boy was *punished* for stealing a watch.

12. **evil** ['ivl̩] *n.* [U] a powerful force that some people believe to exist, and which cause wicked and bad things to happen 罪惡

There is always a conflict between good and *evil* in his mind.

13. **legend** ['lɛdʒənd] *n.* [C] an old, well-known story, often about brave people, adventures, or magical events 傳奇

There are a lot of *legends* in China.

14. **welcome** ['wɛlkəm] *vt.* to accept a person, suggestion, etc. happily 歡迎

The President *welcomed* the Queen as she got off the plane.

15. **parade** [pə'red] *n.* [C] a public procession 遊行

My sister saw a big *parade* on the street yesterday.

16. **march** [mɑrtʃ] *vi.* to walk in a military manner with a regular tread 進行;行軍

They *marched* 30 km. across the foothills.

B. Idioms & Phrases

1. **such as** used when giving an example of something　例如

   I would like to have a cup of drink *such as* tea or coffee.

2. **come from** to have started, been produced or first existed in a particular place, thing or time　來自

   Where does John *come from* originally?

3. **develop from** to gradually begin to have a quality, problem, etc.　發展

   It *develops from* a seed into a big tree in less than 15 years.

C. Word Forms

1. $\text{v.} + \begin{cases} \text{-ance} \\ \text{-ence} \end{cases} \rightarrow \text{n.}$

enter（進入）	→	entrance（入口）
depend（依靠）	→	dependence（依靠）

 The President made a special ***appearance*** on television last night.

He ***appeared*** very calm, but his news was serious.

2. **adj. + -ity → n.**

Christian（基督教的）	→	Christianity（基督教）
popular（流行的）	→	popularity（流行）

England and the United States are **similar** because the people speak the same language.

However, culturally, there are fewer **similarities** and many differences.

1. I'm looking forward to the new actor's first _____ (perform) tonight.
2. Harriet would like to quit her job and go back to school full time, but the _____ (real) of the situation is that she has to continue working.
3. Connie made extra copies of her house keys and gave them to me as a sort of _____ (insure).

D. Sentence Patterns

1. $$\begin{cases} \text{Although} + S_1 + VP_1 + ..., S_2 + VP_2 + ... \\ S_1 + VP_1 + ... + \text{although} + S_2 + VP_2 + ... \end{cases} \text{（雖然）}$$

 Although mistletoe was never used as an official part of Christian celebrations, many British people still pin a sprig of it over a fireplace.

(1) **Although** Jack is not handsome, there is something agreeable in his manner.

(2) He is very strong **although** he is old.

2. $\begin{cases} \text{As} + S_1 + VP_1 + ..., S_2 + VP_2 + ... \\ S_1 + VP_1 + ... + \text{as} + S_2 + VP_2 + ... \end{cases}$ （當…之時）

 As Christianity spread, St. Nicholas replaced Odin in the solstice legends.

(1) She came up **as** I was speaking.

(2) **As** the President began to speak, there was a loud explosion.

 牛刀小試

1. Archer trembled _____ he spoke.

  (a) at (b) as (c) in (d) although

2. _____ Jessica doesn't spend much time studying, she always gets high scores.

3. 當老師正在講課時，約翰睡著了。

  John fell asleep _____ the teacher was lecturing.

 **. Exercise**

I. True/False: *Decide true (T) or false (F) of the following statements based on the text.*

❶ The ways to celebrate Christmas have changed a lot since it replaced Saturnalia.

❷ Mistletoe was never used as an official part of Christian celebrations.

❸ In Australia there is still a festival of St Nicholas on 6 December.

❹ On Christmas midnight children wake eagerly to see if Santa Claus has left them a special gift.

❺ Christmas is also a time for public celebrations in countries with warm climates.

II. Vocabulary Review: *Complete the sentences with the following words of appropriate forms.*

replace	tradition	punish	local	official
welcome	custom	reward	ancient	entrance

❶ It is the _____ for Japanese to bow when they meet their friends.

❷ Getting married before 25 years old is a _____ in his family.

❸ Jones spends much time in researching _____ civilizations.

❹ Nothing can _____ parents' love.

❺ That poor man always stands at the _____ of the theater.

❻ The residents usually go shopping in the _____ supermarkets.

❼ Mother prepared a lot of food to _____ the guests from Japan.

❽ His mother _____ him for the mistake he had made.

❾ The lady didn't accept my application unless I provided the _____ documents.

❿ The kind woman gave me a _____ for saving her child from the fire.

III. Multiple Choice: *Choose the most appropriate word based on the meaning of the context.*

❶ Nobody knows where the old man came _____ .

  (a) from   (b) for   (c) on   (d) in

❷ We need some furniture for our new house such _____ sofa, table, and cabinet.

  (a) for   (b) about   (c) as   (d) with

❸ Plants develop _____ seeds.

  (a) with   (b) into   (c) on   (d) from

❹ The student's attitude toward the teacher has _____ a lot after the teacher spent lots of time talking with him.

  (a) changed   (b) got   (c) received   (d) honoured

❺ Small green plants are usually used _____ the decorations in living rooms.

   (a) as   (b) for   (c) about   (d) at

IV. Cloze Test: *Fill in the blanks with the most appropriate words based on the meaning of the context.*

From Saturnalia came the traditions of feasting, ^{1}_____ parties and decorating homes with evergreen ^{2}_____ such as holly and ivy — a reminder ^{3}_____ even at midwinter the ^{4}_____ of nature survived. When Christianity ^{5}_____ to northern Europe, the missionaries found that the Celts and ^{6}_____ local tribes also honoured the ^{7}_____ at the winter solstice.

V. Translation: *Translate the following Chinese sentences into English.*

❶ 在聖誕節,很多英國人仍然會在壁爐或是家門口掛一小枝檞寄生。

_____

❷ 其他聖誕節的習俗來自於北歐。

_____

❸ 在冬至時,天神奧丁會到地球來訪,以獎勵好人及懲罰惡人。

_____

❹ 許多基督教徒在聖誕夜時,會到教堂參加特別的慶祝儀式。

_____

❺ 在聖誕節早上,孩子們會急著起床,要看看聖誕老公公是否送給他們特別的禮物。

_____

VI. Discussion Topics: *Discuss the following topics on "Christmas" in oral or written reports.*

❶ What do you usually do on Christmas Eve?

❷ Do you believe in the existence of Santa Claus? Why or why not?

❸ Please describe the most unforgettable Christmas you had.

Outside Reading

Valentine's Day

In many countries, Valentine's Day, February 14, is celebrated as a special day for lovers. The day is named in honor of Valentine, a third-century Roman priest who was put to death by the Roman government for disobeying an emergency law that forbade marriages. These days, people in many parts of the world honor Valentine's name by declaring and expressing their love to boy- and girl-friends, husbands and wives, and even classmates.

One of the ways people express caring for their sweethearts is by buying gifts for them. People buy engagement rings, wedding rings, and other jewelry to give to their lovers, sometimes as parts of marriage proposals. Others buy chocolates (said to inspire passion), champagne, and roses for their lovers. Jewelry stores, department stores, and florists do a great business around Valentine's Day.

Restaurants, too, do a booming business at this time of year. Unless you've made reservations, February 14 is not a good day to go out for a quick dinner at your favorite restaurant. Restaurants in many parts of the world are packed with lovers celebrating their special day. Millions of couples go out to dinner, and perhaps to a movie, concert, or other performance.

If there's any single thing that really captures the feeling of Valentine's Day as a day to communicate love, it's the Valentine's Day card. Card-shops prepare weeks in advance, making sure they have cards

that express just the right feeling. Valentine's Day cards express every form of love, from the most passionate to the most innocent. Valentine's Day cards are given by men, women, and children, to people they love, people they hope will like them, or even just people who happen to be classmates. Even in primary schools, children can be seen cutting out paper hearts, pasting them onto cards of every shape and size, stuffing the cards into envelopes, and addressing them to their classmates, boy- and girl-friends, teachers, and parents.

Reading Comprehension

1. Valentine's Day is celebrated in many countries on _____ .

   (a) February 14   (b) July 7   (c) December 24

2. Valentine gets its name from a _____ .

   (a) Greek goddess   (b) French queen   (c) Roman priest

3. As a Valentine's Day gift, _____ are said to inspire passion.

   (a) chocolates   (b) rings   (c) roses

4. Weeks before Valentine's Day, _____ are ordered from florists.

   (a) lilies   (b) sunflowers   (c) roses

5. Valentine's Day cards can be given to _____ .

   (a) lovers   (b) classmates   (c) Both of the above.

English Learning Strategy

I find the meaning of an English word by dividing it into parts that I understand.（我會將一個英文字拆解成可理解的數部份，以便找出其意義。）

carelessness ＝ care ＋ -less ＋ -ness
　（粗心）　（小心）（否定字尾）（名詞字尾）

Carelessness
＝
Care＋less＋ness

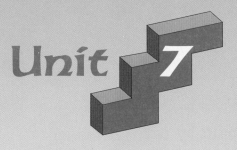

Unit 7

Time Difference

Several years ago my wife, my two children and I decided to **tour**[1] Spain by car. We **hired**[2] a car in Paris and drove down to Perpignan. The following day we crossed the
5 Pyrenees and entered Spain.

After a long day's drive, we found ourselves at about six o'clock in the evening in a small town some distance to the south of Barcelona. We began to *look for* a place to
10 spend our first night in Spain. We soon found a small hotel and *booked in*. Our room was on the first floor. It was small but comfortable and it **contained**[3] a shower.

After we had *freshened* ourselves *up*, I
15 went downstairs to see what **arrangements**[4] I could make for an evening meal. I was sure that there was a restaurant in the hotel, but I did not expect it to be open yet, as I knew that Spanish people eat much later than we do in
20 England. Sure enough, on the ground floor there was a restaurant and a bar. The bar was open, but the restaurant was not. A **notice**[5] on

tour [tʊr]

hire [haɪr]

contain [kənˈten]

arrangement

[əˈrendʒmənt]

notice [ˈnotɪs]

fetch [fɛtʃ]

drive [draɪv]

terrace [ˈtɛrɪs]

firmly [ˈfɜˑmlɪ]

eventually [ɪˈvɛntʃʊəlɪ]

hesitation [ˌhɛzəˈteʃən]

irony [ˈaɪrənɪ]

gradually [ˈgrædʒʊəlɪ]

attitude [ˈætəˌtjud]

flexible [ˈflɛksəbl]

the restaurant door announced that it would open at half past eight. I went and **fetched**[6] my wife and children. Since it was only just past seven o'clock and we were hungry and thirsty after our long **drive**,[7] we decided to *sit on* the **terrace**[8] outside the bar and order a snack and a drink while we *waited for* the restaurant to open.

Time passed, but the doors of the restaurant remained **firmly**[9] closed. Eight-thirty came and went, but there was no sign of the restaurant opening. **Eventually**,[10] at nine o'clock, I asked the waiter what time the restaurant opened. He answered without the slightest **hesitation**[11] and without **irony**[12] that it opened at eight-thirty.

This was our first experience of what we **gradually**[13] came to *refer to* as 'Spanish time'. The Spanish **attitude**[14] towards time is much more **flexible**[15] than that of the

25

30

35

40

45   English. In the beginning, we felt **frustrated**[16] at the **delay**[17] in getting things done and at people's lack of concern for time. However, *before long* we came to see that Spanish people march to the beat of a different drum. *That is*

50   *to say*, they have different **priorities**.[18] To them, there is more to life than **promptness**[19] and they refuse to be the slaves of time. Gradually, the wise visitor relaxes like his hosts and enjoys life.

frustrated [ˈfrʌstretɪd]

delay [dɪˈle]

priority [praɪˈɔrətɪ]

promptness

     [ˈprɑmptnɪs]

 **. Vocabulary**

1. **tour** [tʊr] *vt.* to visit somewhere on a tour　旅行

    They are *touring* France this winter.

2. **hire** [haɪr] *vt.* to purchase the temporary use of (a thing) 雇用

    We don't have enough money to *hire* a car.

3. **contain** [kən'ten] *vt.* to have something inside, or have something as a part　含有

    This letter *contained* important information about Mr. Brown's background.

4. **arrangement** [ə'rendʒmənt] *n.* [C] things that you must organize so that an event, meeting, etc. can happen　安排

    The local newspaper made *arrangements* for an interview with that musician.

5. **notice** ['notɪs] *n.* [C] a displayed sheet etc. bearing an announcement　佈告

    That *notice* on the wall says "No Parking."

6. **fetch** [fɛtʃ] *vt.* to go for and bring back　帶來

    Would you mind going to *fetch* my kids from school?

7. **drive** [draɪv] *n.* [C] a trip in a car　駕車

    We planned to go for a *drive* along the coast.

8. **terrace** ['tɛrɪs] *n.* [C] an area, especially next to a hotel or restaurant, where people can sit outside to eat or drink　陽臺

    Our neighbors had a picnic on the *terrace* yesterday.

9. **firmly** ['fɝmlɪ] *adv.* strongly or securely　堅固地

All the doors and windows are *firmly* shut.

10. **eventually** [ɪˈvɛntʃʊəlɪ] *adv.* after a long time   最後

Jeff worked so hard that *eventually* he made himself ill.

11. **hesitation** [ˌhɛzəˈteʃən] *n.* [U] indecision; pause in doubt   遲疑

The boy followed that young man without *hesitation*.

12. **irony** [ˈaɪrənɪ] *n.* [U] the use of words that are the opposite of what you really mean   諷刺

Jack called the foolish boy "genius" in *irony*.

13. **gradually** [ˈgrædʒʊəlɪ] *adv.* in a way that happens or develops slowly over a long period of time   逐漸地

Gradually the father tried to understand his son.

14. **attitude** [ˈætəˌtjud] *n.* [C] the opinions and feelings that you usually have about someone or something   態度

Joe's *attitude* towards women really scares me.

15. **flexible** [ˈflɛksəbl̩] *adj.* adaptable; variable   彈性的；可通融的

Mom said that we can be *flexible* about our schedule.

16. **frustrated** [ˈfrʌstretɪd] *adj.* discontented because unable to achieve one's aims   挫折的

Mark gets *frustrated* when he can't win.

17. **delay** [dɪˈle] *n.* [C] postponement; deferment   遲延

We are very sorry for the *delay*, Mr. Carlson.

18. **priority** [praɪˈɔrətɪ] *n.* [C] the thing that you think is most important and that needs attention before anything else   優先順序

In the past, women's issues are often seen as a low *priority*.

19. **promptness** [ˈprɑmptnɪs] *n.* [U] the state of being done quickly and immediately   敏捷；快速

That express company always emphasizes the *promptness* of its delivery.

B. Idioms & Phrases

1. **look for** to find a particular kind of thing or person that you need or want 尋找

   The policeman is still *looking for* the prisoner who escaped two days ago.

2. **book in** to arrive at a hotel and say who you are etc. 登記

   I promise I'll call you as soon as I *book in* at my hotel.

3. **freshen up** to wash your hands and face in order to feel clean and comfortable 使清爽

   Aileen hurried into the bathroom to *freshen up* before the meeting.

4. **sit on** to be on a chair or seat, or on the ground 坐

   Joy is *sitting on* the chair in her office.

5. **wait for** not to do something or go somewhere until something else happens 等待

   I've been *waiting for* you all day! Where were you?

6. **refer to** to mention or speak about someone or something 說到

   The two brothers agreed never to *refer to* the matter again.

7. **before long** soon 不久

   Before long Bill took over the editing of the magazine.

8. **that is to say** about to express the same idea more clearly 也就是說

   I'm hungry. *That is to say*, I need something to eat.

 . **Word Forms**

1. **adj. + -en → v.**

        fresh（清爽的）   →   freshen（使清爽）
        broad（寬廣的）   →   broaden（使寬廣）

 The government will not ***widen*** the old highway, although it is too narrow.
Instead, the government is planning a new highway, which will be very ***wide***.

2. **adj. + -ness → n.**

        prompt（快速的） →   promptness（快速）
        shy（害羞的）   →   shyness（害羞）

 The teacher left school early because she felt ***ill*** during class.
Fortunately, her ***illness*** seemed to improve by the next morning.

1. Next semester Betty will _____ (broad) her major in foreign languages. She plans to study Spanish and Portuguese as well as French.
2. My father finally went to the doctor because his _____ (sleepless) was so severe.
3. My aunt overcame her _____ (lonely) by going out more often with her friends.

D. Sentence Patterns

1. $S_1 + VP_1 + $ 疑問詞 $ + S_2 + VP_2$（間接問句）

what, which, who, when, where, why, how, whose, whom 等疑問詞所引導的直接問句改為間接問句時，疑問句內的主詞和動詞不倒裝。

 I went downstairs to see **what** arrangements **I could make** for an evening meal.

(1) Please tell me **where Jane lives**.

(2) I am going to find out **what Tom bought** last night.

2. more + Adj. + than + $\begin{cases} \text{that} \\ \text{those} \end{cases}$ of + ...

Time Difference

比較級句型為了避免同一名詞的重複，可用 that 代替前面已提過之單數名詞，用 those 代替前面已提過之複數名詞。

 The Spanish attitude towards time is much ***more flexible than that of*** the English.

(1) The climate of Taiwan is ***warmer than that of*** Japan.

(2) My paintings are ***more colorful than those of*** yours.

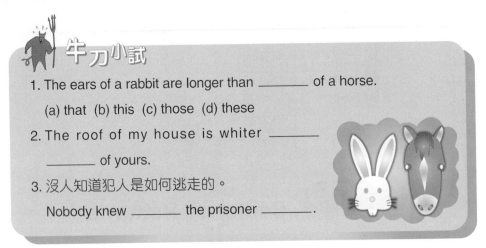

牛刀小試

1. The ears of a rabbit are longer than _____ of a horse.

   (a) that (b) this (c) those (d) these

2. The roof of my house is whiter _____
   _____ of yours.

3. 沒人知道犯人是如何逃走的。
   Nobody knew _____ the prisoner _____.

. Exercise

I. True/False: *Decide true (T) or false (F) of the following statements based on the text.*

❶ After their long drive, the author's family arrived in a small town near Perpignan.

❷ The author's family stayed in a large and comfortable hotel room.

❸ The author did not expect the restaurant to be open when they booked in.

❹ The restaurant did not open at half past eight.

❺ Promptness is the first priority for Spanish people.

II. Vocabulary Review: *Complete the sentences with the following words of appropriate forms.*

distance	delay	downstairs	flexible	thirsty
attitude	refuse	hesitate	contain	slave

❶ Don't _____ to write to her.

❷ The building _____ two restaurants and twenty offices.

❸ It is a long _____ from my home to the train station.

❹ Please go _____ and lock the front door.

❺ Cathy told me her father was once a _____ of drink.

❻ There was a _____ before he began to speak.

❼ I was _____ after one-hour exercise.

❽ What is Mother's _____ to the problem?

❾ My sister works _____ hours.

❿ Jane _____ to accept the company's invitation.

III. Multiple Choice: *Choose the most appropriate word based on the meaning of the context.*

❶ The professor frequently refers _____ the Bible.

   (a) to   (b) in   (c) of   (d) with

❷ Jenny looked in her bag _____ her house key but could not find it.

   (a) at   (b) about   (c) on   (d) for

❸ _____ long Roy and Helen got married.

   (a) After   (b) Before (c) Still   (d) Between

❹ Kevin is waiting _____ my final decision.

   (a) on   (b) for   (c) to   (d) about

❺ The little girl is sitting _____ his father's shoulder.

   (a) in   (b) at   (c) on   (d) to

IV. Cloze Test: *Fill in the blanks with the most appropriate words based on the meaning*

of the context.

After we had freshened ourselves ^{1}_____ , I went downstairs to see what arrangements I could ^{2}_____ for an evening meal. The bar was open, ^{3}_____ the restaurant was not. A ^{4}_____ on the restaurant door announced that it would open at half ^{5}_____ eight. We decided to sit on the terrace outside the bar and ^{6}_____ a snack and a drink while we waited ^{7}_____ the restaurant to open.

V. Translation: *Translate the following Chinese sentences into English.*

❶ 幾年前，我和我太太及兩個小孩，決定以開車方式遊覽西班牙。

_____

❷ 時間過去了，但是餐廳的門仍然緊閉著。

_____

❸ 侍者毫不遲疑並不帶一絲諷刺地回答說，餐廳在八點三十分開始營業。

_____

❹ 西班牙人對時間的態度較英國人彈性多了。

_____

❺ 一開始，我們因人們缺乏時間觀念而感到沮喪。

_____

VI. Discussion Topics: *Discuss the following topics on "time" in oral or written reports.*

❶ Please describe "Spanish time."

❷ Is the Chinese attitude towards time more like that of the English or the Spanish? Why?

❸ Are you usually early, punctual, or late for a class? How about a date?

Outside Reading

Procrastination

The verb *procrastinate* comes from the Latin *procrastinare*, which means "to postpone until tomorrow." To procrastinate, then, is to delay doing something until some future time. A procrastinator is someone who is always putting off what he or she should be doing right now.

Those of us who have a tendency toward procrastination know that it is a terrible habit. Every day, we tell ourselves that we must start doing things immediately. Every day, we postpone our work, miss deadlines, and break promises. Because we always procrastinate, we are always trying to catch up. We are always doing yesterday's jobs today, and today's jobs tomorrow.

There are people who rarely procrastinate. They are highly efficient and well organized. They seem to get everything done on time. I suspect that they never leave home in the morning before they make the bed, never go to sleep at night before they finish their work, and are never late for appointments. As a result, they are probably always one step ahead of you and me.

Maybe the way to overcome procrastination is to change our habits gradually. We can start with a daily schedule of the things we need to accomplish. But let's be reasonable. We shouldn't crowd the list with too many tasks. We should be realistic about what we can do. Especially in the beginning, we should be lenient with ourselves. After all, if we fail at the start, we will get discouraged and go right back to our old habits.

Reading Comprehension

1. The verb procrastinate comes from a _____ word.

   (a) French   (b) German   (c) Latin

2. A procrastinator is always doing _____ jobs today.

   (a) yesterday's   (b) today's   (c) tomorrow's

3. According to the author, procrastination is a _____ habit.

   (a) good   (b) rare   (c) terrible

4. According to the author, there are people who _____ procrastinate.

   (a) seldom   (b) often   (c) always

5. Which of the following is NOT true when we start with a daily schedule?

   (a) Be reasonable.   (b) Be ambitious.   (c) Be realistic.

English Learning Strategy

To understand unfamiliar English words, I make guesses.
（我會去猜測英文生字的意義。）

Unit 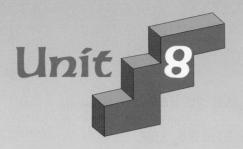 8

Answering Machines

*Hello. This is Susan. I'm not able to answer the phone right now. After the **beep**,[1] please leave your name and number, and I'll get back to you as soon as I can.*

Nowadays, it is very common to hear messages like this on people's answering machines. *Because of* the increasing **pace**[2] of life, **irregular**[3] work **schedules**,[4] and away-
5 from-home **leisure**[5] activities, many people use answering machines *so that* they don't miss important calls when they are out. Like **cassette**[6] recorders, answering machines record messages so that when a person arrives
10 home, he or she can simply replay the cassette and *find out* who has called. Some newer answering machines store messages on a computer **chip**[7] instead of an audiotape.

    Many other ways of **relaying**[8] messages
15 have been developed out of the need for **immediate**[9] communication. A little less impersonal than an answering machine is an answering service. For a monthly fee, phone calls can be **rerouted**[10] to an agency in which a
20 clerk *takes down* the name, number, and message of the caller. The customer can call the service any time from anywhere and

beep [bip]

pace [pes]

irregular [ɪˈrɛgjələ˞]

schedule [ˈskɛdʒul]

leisure [ˈliʒə˞]

cassette [kəˈsɛt]

chip [tʃɪp]

relay [rɪˈle]

immediate [ɪˈmidɪɪt]

reroute [rɪˈrut]

receive messages. Still another way to get phone messages is call-forwarding—rerouting calls to an alternate number, such as one's 25 workplace or health club. A caller dialing a home number **automatically**[11] reaches another number where the person has **forwarded**[12] his or her calls.

automatically

[ˌɔtə'mætɪkļɪ]

forward ['fɔrwəd]

The fact that telephones are *no longer* 30 limited to *how far* the cord will reach is a **distinct**[13] advantage. Cordless, battery-operated models enable people to carry phones to different rooms of the house and use them in their yards, cars, and boats. 35 *Cellular phones* with **antennas**[14] can be **installed**[15] in cars and are able to **transmit**[16] calls using a system of transmitters placed throughout a given area. Other cellular phones can be carried anywhere in a small bag, and 40 new models called flip-phones are so small they can fit in your pocket.

distinct [dɪ'stɪŋkt]

antenna [æn'tɛnə]

install [ɪn'stɔl]

transmit [træns'mɪt]

Another device is the beeper, so *named for* the type of signal it emits. Because a beeper

45 fits comfortably into a pocket or on a belt, it is
used **extensively**[17] by people who spend their
workday in many different locations, such as
medical **personnel**[18] and home repair people.
The beeping signal is heard when a certain

50 number is dialed. People carrying beepers
know that they must *call* somebody *back* to
find out why they were beeped.

All these variations on the telephone prove
that although a hundred years have passed

55 since its invention, the telephone is still our
most important **means**[19] of personal
communication.

extensively

[ɪkˈstɛnsɪvlɪ]

personnel [ˌpɝsn̩ˈɛl]

means [minz]

A. Vocabulary

1. **beep** [bip] *n.* [C] a short high sound made by an electronic machine　嗶聲

   Please leave your message after the *beep*.

2. **pace** [pes] *n.* [C] the rate or speed at which something happens or at which someone does something　步調

   Eddie likes to work at his own *pace*.

3. **irregular** [ɪˋrɛgjələ] *adj.* not regular　無規律的

   Shirley's attendance at school has been somewhat *irregular*.

4. **schedule** [ˋskɛdʒul] *n.* [C] a plan of work　時間表

   We'll let you know if the *schedule* is changed.

5. **leisure** [ˋliʒə] *n.* [U] time when you are not working or studying and can relax and do things you enjoy　空閒

   In my *leisure* time I listen to music and play piano.

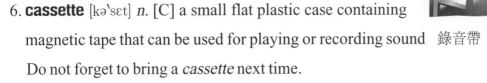

6. **cassette** [kəˋsɛt] *n.* [C] a small flat plastic case containing magnetic tape that can be used for playing or recording sound　錄音帶

   Do not forget to bring a *cassette* next time.

7. **chip** [tʃɪp] *n.* [C] a small piece of silicon that has a set of complicated electrical connections on it and is used to store and process　晶片

   This kind of *chip* is used to control "intelligent" machines such as televisions.

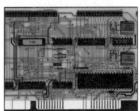

8. **relay** [rɪˋle] *vt.* to receive (a message, broadcast, etc.) and transmit it to others 轉播;轉寄

Please *relay* this fax message to my secretary.

9. **immediate** [ɪˋmidɪɪt] *adj.* occurring or done at once 即時的

Your *immediate* answer to our question will be appreciated.

10. **reroute** [rɪˋrut] *vt.* to send or carry by a different route 改變行程

The usual route cannot be used so the flight schedule has to be *rerouted*.

11. **automatically** [ˌɔtəˋmætɪklɪ] *adv.* working by itself, without direct human intervention 自動地

The door would open *automatically* when you push this button.

12. **forward** [ˋfɔrwəˋd] *vt.* to send on to a further destination 轉遞

Do not forget to *forward* this letter to my parents, please.

13. **distinct** [dɪˋstɪŋkt] *adj.* clearly perceptible 顯著的

The outline of the big ship became more *distinct*.

14. **antenna** [ænˋtɛnə] *n.* [C] a wire used for receiving radio or television signals 天線

The engineer used radio *antennas* for satellite communication.

15. **install** [ɪnˋstɔl] *vt.* to place (equipment etc.) in position ready for use 安裝

Do you know how to *install* this meter on the bicycle?

16. **transmit** [trænsˋmɪt] *vt.* to transfer 傳送

The information is electronically *transmitted* to schools and colleges.

17. **extensively** [ɪkˋstɛnsɪvlɪ] *adv.* covering a large area 廣大地

Despite reading *extensively*, she still failed the exam.

18. **personnel** [ˌpɝsṇˋɛl] *n.* [U] staff of an organization, the armed forces, a public service, etc. 人員

All *personnel* are required to pay the insurance fee.

19. **means** [minz] *n.* [C] a method, system, or object that you use as a way of achieving a result 方法

What would be the most effective *means* of traveling around the city?

B. Idioms & Phrases

1. **right now** at the moment 現在

   I am busy *right now*. I'll call you back 10 minutes later.

2. **as soon as** immediately after something has happened 一⋯就⋯

   I'll call you *as soon as* I arrive.

3. **because of** as a result of a particular thing or of someone's actions 由於

   Because of the rain, we could not go outside.

4. **so that** in order that 為了⋯（表目的）

   Joseph brings a laptop computer with him *so that* he can get on the internet any time.

5. **find out** to learn information after trying to discover it 發現

   She worked hard to *find out* the problems.

6. **take down** to write something down 寫下；記下

   A secretary needs to learn how to *take down* important information efficiently.

7. **no longer** used when something used to happen in the past but does not happen now 不再

   Susan *no longer* works for this company from today.

8. **how far** used when asking the distance between two places 多遠

   I have no idea *how far* we have traveled today.

9. **cellular phone** a telephone that you can carry around with you 行動電話

Nowadays you can buy a *cellular phone* with a very low price.

10. **name for** to give someone or something a particular name 取名

This college is *named for* Carlson School.

11. **call back** to telephone someone again, especially because you were not in when he or she called 回電

Please tell him I'll *call back* later.

C . Word Forms

1. **adj. + -ity → n.**

active（活動的） → activity（活動）

 Contrary to popular myth, ***senility*** is not an inevitable part of becoming older.

In fact, most older people never become at all ***senile***, and their minds remain sharp and clear.

2. **en- + { adj. / n. → v.**

able（有能力的） → enable（使能夠）

 You don't have the ***courage*** to walk into the building.

I do not ***encourage*** you to do that.

 牛刀小試

1. He developed this mechanical _____ (able) by working in his father's factory.

2. She would like to go to school full time, but the _____ (real) of the situation is that she has no money.

3. I _____ (counter) an old lady named Jean on the street.

D. Sentence Patterns

1. $\begin{cases} \text{Because} + S_1 + VP_1, S_2 + VP_2 \\ \text{because of} + \text{N.P.} \end{cases}$ （因為）

 Because of the increasing pace of life, irregular work schedules, and away-from-home leisure activities, many people use answering machines so that they don't miss important calls when they are out.

Because a beeper fits comfortably into a pocket or on a belt, it is used extensively by people who spend their workday in many different locations, such as medical personnel and home repair people.

(1) **Because** I'm busy, I can't go.

(2) I didn't go out **because of** the rain.

2. S₁ + VP₁ + so that + S₂ + Aux. + 原形 V.（為了…）

 Many people use answering machines **so that** they don't miss important calls when they are out.

Like cassette recorders, answering machines record messages **so that** when a person arrives home, he or she can simply replay the cassette and find out who has called.

(1) Judy studies hard **so that** she may pass the test.

(2) Eric got up early yesterday **so that** he might catch the plane.

牛刀小試

1. He will succeed, _____ he does his best.

2. Most people love John _____ _____ his kindness.

3. Switch the light _____ _____ I can see what color it is.

. Exercise

I. True/False: *Decide true (T) or false (F) of the following statements based on the text.*

❶ Some newer answering machines store messages on an audiotape rather than a computer chip.

❷ An answering service is more personal than an answering machine.

❸ The customer can call the service any time from anywhere and receive messages.

❹ Telephones are still limited to how far the cord will reach.

❺ The telephone is still our most important means of personal communication.

II. Vocabulary Review: *Complete the sentences with the following words of appropriate forms.*

battery	store	device	beeper	antenna
leisure	communication	install	forward	emit

❶ I have no _____ time to read novels.

❷ Americans often _____ the furniture in the attic.

❸ Human beings _____ with one another by various instruments.

❹ We _____ air-conditioner in a house when it is hot.

❺ Anne always keeps dry _____ for emergency.

❻ Your letter will be _____ to me from my former address.

❼ People sometimes keep a _____ so that others can reach them easily.

❽ Due to the damages of the _____ , I can't get through my sister's cellular phone.

❾ I hope someday I can invent a new _____ for catching cockroaches.

❿ When Annie thinks of her mother in the hospital, she _____ a sigh.

III. Multiple Choice: *Choose the most appropriate word based on the meaning of the context.*

❶ Judy called me when I was out, so she left a message _____ my answering machine.

    (a) at   (b) to   (c) on   (d) in

❷ Kevin is named _____ the class president this semester.

    (a) in   (b) for   (c) at   (d) of

❸ The nurse in the clinic usually takes _____ the patients' names first.

    (a) out   (b) up   (c) to   (d) down

❹ A visit to the moon is _____ longer a dream.

(a) all   (b) every   (c) any   (d) no

❺ Steve is trying to find _____ how long the river really is.

(a) out   (b) in   (c) up   (d) of

IV. Cloze Test: *Fill in the blanks with the most appropriate words based on the meaning of the context.*

Many other ways of relaying messages have [1]_____ developed out of the need for immediate [2]_____ . For a monthly [3]_____ , phone calls can be rerouted to an agency in which a clerk takes [4]_____ the name, number, and message of the caller. The customer can call the service any time from [5]_____ and receive messages. Still another way to get phone messages is call-forwarding—rerouting calls to an alternate number. A caller [6]_____ a home number automatically reaches another number where the person has [7]_____ his or her calls.

V. Translation: *Translate the following Chinese sentences into English.*

❶ 很多人使用電話答錄機，如此一來，他們不在時也不會錯過重要的電話。

_____

❷ 電話不再受限於電話線所能到達的距離是個獨特的優點。

_____

❸ 裝有天線的行動電話也能安裝在汽車裡。

_____

❹ 呼叫器是以它所發出的訊號而命名。

_____

❺ 帶呼叫器的人知道他們一定要回電，才能曉得他們為什麼被呼叫。

_____

VI. Discussion Topics: *Discuss the following topics on "answering machine" in oral or written reports.*

❶ If the person you call is out, will you leave your message on the answering machine? Why or why not?

❷ What are the advantages of using an answering machine? Are there also disadvantages?

❸ If there were no telephones, what would life become?

Outside Reading

Always Return Your Phone Calls

All you need is love.

John Lennon

Angela knew that Charlotte, her best friend, was having a rough time. Charlotte was moody and depressed. She was withdrawn around everyone except for Angela. She instigated arguments with her mom and had violent confrontations with her sister. Most of all, Charlotte's bleak and desperate poetry worried Angela.

No one was on particularly good speaking terms with Charlotte that summer. For most of her friends, Charlotte had become too difficult. They had no interest in hanging out with someone who was so bleak and in so much pain. Their attempts to "be a friend" were met with angry accusations or depressed indifference.

Angela was the only one who could reach her. Although she would have liked to be outside, Angela spent most of her time inside with her troubled friend. Then a day came when Angela had to move. She was going just across town, but Charlotte would no longer be her neighbor, and they would be spending far less time together.

The first day in her new neighborhood, out playing with her new neighbors, Angela wondered how Charlotte was doing. When she got home, shortly before twilight, her mother told her Charlotte had called.

Angela went to the phone to return the call. No answer. She left a message on

Charlotte's machine. "Hi Charlotte, it's Angela. Call me back."

About half an hour later Charlotte called. "Angela, I have to tell you something. When you called, I was in the basement. I had a gun to my head. I was about to kill myself, but then I heard your voice on the machine upstairs."

Angela collapsed into her chair.

"When I heard your voice I realized someone loves me, and I am so lucky that it is you. I'm going to get help, because I love you, too."

Charlotte hung up the phone. Angela went right over to Charlotte's house, and they sat on the porch swing and cried.

Reading Comprehension

1. Charlotte was Angela's _____ .

   (a) classmate   (b) roommate   (c) best friend

2. Charlotte had violent confrontations with _____ .

   (a) Angela   (b) her mom   (c) her sister

3. Why has Charlotte become too difficult for most of her friends?

   (a) She was so talkative.   (b) She was so bleak.   (c) She was so excited.

4. _____ was the only one who could reach Charlotte.

   (a) Angela   (b) Charlotte's mom   (c) Charlotte's sister

5. Charlotte was going to _____ when Angela returned her call on the answering machine.

   (a) call Angela   (b) kill herself   (c) go to Angela's house

English Learning Strategy

I read English without looking up every new word.（閱讀英文時，我不會碰到每個生字都去查字典。）

Index I

Vocabulary

123

Index II

Idioms & Phrases